12 dates till christmas

KENDRA MASE

THE CHAMPAGNE HIT ME FIRST. No, wait. It was probably the espresso martini Gina had made, the one she swore she'd perfected as she shook together leftover salted-caramel vodka and pumpkin spice liqueur.

I regretted it the second it touched my tongue.

Because the worst part?

It actually tasted good.

Maybe it was the cup she had put it in that threw me off. It was a commemorative Metropolitan Museum of Art mug, chipped on one side—the kind they sold in the gift shop for twenty bucks, but Gina had claimed was a badge of honor. She'd earned it on her last day as a summer intern, one of only six picked from hundreds.

Of course, she also left with a shiny new line for her résumé and a summer full of existential dread about her future. That part had been free.

Now, two master's degrees later—hers in art history slash museum studies and mine in writing with a concentration in both creative nonfiction and technical communication for *balance*—we'd managed to delay the inevitable adulthood just long enough for the real world to feel like a complete ambush.

But we were doing it. Somehow. Oddly, together.

In a stroke of chaotic timing that felt weirdly cinematic, we were living out the very dream we had scribbled into notebook margins when we were thirteen. We were two best friends, grown up and living in the city, chasing creative careers and sharing a too-small apartment with questionable plumbing. We even had our own "quirky neighbor" subplot in the form of Gina's older brother crashing with us semi-permanently.

It wasn't glamorous. But it was ours.

Gina was thriving. At least, she was faking it really well. Which, in her opinion, was the same thing. She had a job at a gallery that had real-name artists and catered parties and clients who said things like "provocative space" and "new, emergent voices" with completely straight faces and she pretended to know what they meant.

Somehow, she made it work. She said she wouldn't settle for anything beneath her. And she didn't.

Meanwhile, I was ready to settle for anyone who could spell my name correctly on a job rejection email. Even if they didn't, I could make it work.

I'd sent out dozens—hundreds?—of résumés. Most of the listings were for glorified office assistants. I was ready to be answering phones, managing calendars, and replenishing the stapler supplies as needed. Though most of them said they required at least a master's degree, which seemed, well ...

"Beneath you," Gina had insisted.

I ignored her words, however well meaning.

It was temporary. I was just paying bills while I chased my real dream. Writing.

Unfortunately, writing turned out to be the most elusive

dream of all. More improbable than Gina's *trust-fund baby* fantasy. At least that'd had a road map.

Writing was sending emails into the void. Pitching articles no one asked for to editors who never responded. I'd tried celebrity gossip pieces I didn't care about. Listicles about table settings for holiday dinners with color-coordinated napkins no one used. I'd missed the Thanksgiving content window entirely. Those pitches went out the second Halloween candy went on clearance. Not to mention Christmas.

That left me with Easter.

Did people even read articles about Easter?

I tried to remember the last time I'd celebrated it.

What surfaced was a hazy scene from childhood. There were pastel eggs hidden under patchy lawn grass, sunlight cutting through the slats of a bent chain-link fence. My father, round in the middle, stood in a polo shirt, laughing. My mother crouched barefoot on painted toes, tight curls haloing her face as she clapped and cheered.

"One more, Bri-Bri! Find one more, baby!"

I held that memory in one hand and the espresso martini in the other, sipping cautiously and trying not to grimace at the aftertaste. Sharp. Like burnt sugar.

Gina had called the night an "apartment-warming," but really, it was an excuse to drink. We'd been in the place three months already.

When I'd told her that, she'd pivoted immediately looking for another, much better reason. "Fine, Friendsgiving."

Her version of a friend-focused Thanksgiving featured a bowl of microwave popcorn, a plate of bodega cookies, and at least six bottles of wine, brought by guests who thought a housewarming gift meant cheap pinot.

We were well stocked until New Year's. Unless our third roommate got to it first.

Josh, Gina's older brother, had appeared shortly after we moved in, trailing a duffel bag, two plastic storage bins labeled *J STUFF*, and a history involving a car accident and a personality transplant.

He hadn't left since.

His bins remained mostly untouched in the corner of the living room, stacked beneath a plastic jack-o'-lantern wrapped in multicolored Christmas lights. A seasonal mash-up he claimed was "a vibe."

The apartment was loud, cluttered, slightly unstable. Much like Gina honestly always was. Like us.

And still, somehow, exactly what we'd always imagined.

Just a little messier.

"He says he's looking for his own place." Gina told me when she warned that he was coming to stay with us just for a few days. But also, he had boxes, which made me think a few days wasn't just a few days at all. "I doubt he'll last until the new year before he's jetting off to someplace or another."

"Didn't he say he got a job?" I asked.

Gina shrugged, knowing better than to count on her brother. "Where did you hear that?"

Josh had missed her past few birthdays and graduations, off finding himself somewhere. She joked she was surprised he'd ever returned.

"We'll see. Just tell me now. One word, and I won't bring it up again. If you don't want him here, he has other friends he can mooch off of. I'll kick him out."

"It's fine," I said.

Though the last time I had seen Gina's brother was Christmas during our first year of college, and, well, I couldn't say that we'd left on optimal terms exactly.

"He did mention helping with the rent," added Gina.

That caught my attention the most. "He said he'd pay rent?"

If anything, it made my decision to be unbothered even clearer. There really was no decision.

"No. It's completely fine," I said as if the entire thing had always been my ideal living scenario. "I'll be out writing all the time."

"Right. And you'll definitely have interviews anyway before getting an amazing job," Gina continued, ever positive.

"I doubt I'll even notice he's here."

"You're the best, Bri."

That, of course, had been over a month ago. And tonight was the first night that our pull-out couch was actually in couch form. In fact, I felt like I rarely saw him since he'd started living here. He was up early for work or to go to the gym and often back late. Maybe, some days, he never returned at all.

Neither of us seemed to want to relive the last grand embarrassment we'd had when we last spoke to each other years ago and continued to happily mooch off the other for minimized rent.

And let Gina throw parties with people we didn't know.

* * *

"Come on, Gina," Brent pressed from across the low table with an expression of gleeful interrogation. He had the easy charm of someone who definitely didn't look like he belonged in HR—button-down shirt wrinkled from the commute, sleeves shoved up to his elbows, his laugh always just a little too loud for workplace decorum. "You've been in the city for months now. There's no way you haven't met someone."

"I didn't say I haven't tried," Gina said with a teasing edge, lifting her glass, but not drinking from it. "You're being nosy."

"So, that's a yes?" Brent clarified, grinning.

Gina shrugged, lazy and casual. "Just someone from my last internship. He moved. It wasn't serious."

" 'Not serious,' " echoed a girl from the other end of the table, making air quotes with dramatic flair of her wrists. She had been in the same internship as Gina. I recognized her face, but not her name, and at this point in the night, I wasn't about to ask. "He was way older than you."

Gina's smile tilted into something both mischievous and unapologetic. "He was fun."

"So was Jocelyn," someone else chimed in, and the table erupted into new laughter.

I watched the conversation bounce back and forth like a ping-pong match, everyone leaning in for the latest volley.

Gina's eyes lit up. "So was Jocelyn," she repeated.

"I still think she was perfect for you," said someone—probably Melanie.

"No, no," Gina said quickly, waving a hand tipped in glossy cream-colored nails, her stack of bracelets sliding with the movement. "We're not talking about me and my ridiculous romantic misadventures."

I couldn't help it; I snorted into my cup.

Like clockwork, Gina's gaze snapped to mine. Her dark eyes had that piercing intensity she used on strangers and stubborn bartenders, but now it was focused squarely on me. I met her look with a warning arch of my brow.

Don't do it.

Too late.

She threw an arm around my shoulders, pulling me into an exaggerated sway that made the room dip more than the wine had already managed. "We should really be talking about my poor, sad, romantic little artist."

"Wait a—Gina, stop." I squirmed out from under her, pushing her away with a half-hearted shove. "I'm not lonely."

"Are you with anyone right now, Brielle?" Melanie asked, practically purring across the table.

"She hasn't been on a date in years!"

"That's such an exaggeration," I said. "I went on a date last semester. During my writing residency, remember?"

The looks around the table said no one remembered. Or they didn't believe me.

Which was a fluke, honestly. Getting into the residency, I mean. Another expensive gamble, dressed up as an opportunity. Another chance to drain money I didn't have, in exchange for bunk beds and soggy cafeteria salads and the privilege of writing stories that weren't going anywhere.

I'd realized that halfway through the trip after a rejection from a well-known literary magazine who was one of many proclaiming my writing just wasn't what they were looking for. The residency unfortunately wasn't going to be some magical leap forward into my writing career. That no one was going to "discover" me. That it might just be another line on a résumé no one would read.

So, yeah, I had gotten a little distracted.

His name was Jimmy. Thirty-eight. Salt-and-pepper hair that he always wore pulled back into a low ponytail with a soft elastic he kept on his wrist. Hair long enough to tug, once, and he had laughed—low, with that amused, knowing sound deep in his throat, like he wasn't surprised, like he'd expected me to do it.

He was writing a nonfiction case study on rural health infrastructure in Appalachia—very serious. He made sure I knew it too, though he'd leave out pages for me to read by the coffee maker in the shared lounge. The pages were heavy. Earnest. Full of numbers and suffering and statistics with no clear solution. His voice in them was calm and compassionate, the kind that made you think he was probably better in writing than in real life.

We weren't really supposed to get involved with each other —technically. But it was one of those unspoken things. The kind that happened when people are trapped in too-close quarters with too many feelings and not enough distractions. It felt inevitable.

It wasn't love. It wasn't even lust. Not really.

It was more like gravity. Like leaning too far in and not catching yourself in time.

He told me once, lying on his back in bed, that I reminded him of someone. He didn't say who. He didn't have to. I thought we both knew I wasn't going to be the person in his story. Just a person. A paragraph maybe. A single striking detail.

Still, there was something about the way he looked at me after I read one of my pieces aloud during the workshop. Like he'd been holding his breath and didn't realize until the end that he started breathing again.

That part I kept.

The rest? I didn't know. We'd slept together a few times. We shared a bottle of bourbon on the porch during a rainstorm. Once, he kissed me in the hallway like it was an apology. Another time, he left early from a critique session without saying goodbye. I thought we both knew it was going nowhere, but still, it felt necessary at the time.

Necessary in the way that mistakes sometimes were, especially when you were pretending you still believed you were going to be a writer, not just a glorified secretary who used to have potential.

Now, it was just a fuzzy blur in my memory. Not unpleasant, just vague. Like when you tried to recall the exact smell of a place you'd only visited once. You remembered the feeling more than the details.

And maybe that was enough. Maybe that was all it was ever supposed to be.

I didn't write about Jimmy afterward.

I told myself I might. That I was saving it—that it needed to settle, steep like tea or bruises. But really, I didn't know what the story was. There was no arc, no revelation, no elegant metaphor to tie it all together. Just a handful of scenes that kept playing in the back of my head, like a film reel slightly out of order. His laugh. His hands. That thing he'd said about my writing voice being "quiet in the way you have to lean in to hear it."

Basically meaning, you had to want to care.

Another one of Gina's new art friends, with the tiny astrological tattoos in the spaces between his knuckles, hissed, "A residency lover doesn't count."

And most people didn't care for the whole story.

"It's like ... an affair," Brent added. "It doesn't count."

"I'm pretty sure affairs count," said Melanie.

"Not like *affairs*, affairs. Like ... *love affairs*? They're stories you get to tell your grandchildren to scandalize them when you're, like, eighty or whatever," Brent said before returning his attention to me.

I had enough issues right now. I didn't need anything from my life to be referenced as "an affair." It sounded dirty.

Gina hugged my shoulders again. This time, I let her. If anything, I needed a little support as we pivoted away from this conversation. "My girl wants a good, sweet man to spoil her."

Or not.

I shook my head. The lighting was dark enough here that no

one had to see my flushed face—and not only from the absurd amount of alcohol in my mug.

"Come on, just have us all set you up with someone," Gina suggested.

"I thought you were on my side."

"I am on your side."

Melanie sighed, leaning over the table, propping her chin in her hand. "The side of love. No, better. *Holiday* love."

"Is that really a thing?"

"Of course it is!"

"All of you want to set me up with the same guy?" I cocked my head at them. Foreheads creased around me at the proposal. "Are we living in a fairy tale now?"

"No." Gina shook her head.

"I don't know," said Brent, blinking down at his cup before taking another sip. "I kind of feel like Gina might've just poisoned us all."

Gina rolled her eyes. "Different guys, Bri. All of us will set you up on a date. One each. Or more, of course, if things go well."

"If you have to find more than a few guys to go out with me, I'm pretty sure things would be going the opposite of well," I murmured.

No one seemed to hear me.

"Did everyone hear that?" asked Gina.

A few more heads—half in our conversation, half in their own—turned to focus on what was being plotted around me.

"That would be, like, a dozen people," I said.

"A dozen *chances*," Gina corrected, as if that made a difference.

That was a lot of chances. So many chances that it would be more than pitiful if none of them made it to a second date.

"You all know that many single guys?"

Melanie opened her mouth—

"Scratch that," I cut her off. "Decent single guys who want to date someone like me?"

"What? You have the plague?" Brent asked.

No, but for some reason, it sure did feel like I had been cursed my entire life, no matter how optimistic I tried to be ... in spurts.

"I'm sure we can pull something together. So, what's the problem?" she asked.

Melanie shrugged next to her. "Girl's gotta have options."

"Like blind dates," Brent agreed.

"Me, on blind dates?" I hiccuped and quickly covered my mouth. Though it appeared that nearly everyone else must've been just as plastered as I was feeling. This was getting out of hand.

No one noticed, except for one of Gina's coworkers behind us on the couch, who remained sober.

She handed me another glass of water.

I offered a wave to her in thanks.

She already had an amused smile. Actually, everyone had a glass of water in front of them now.

What would we do without this new friend I didn't know the name of?

"I shouldn't be worried about guys right now," I said.

"But aren't you?"

I didn't answer. Was I slightly worried that, eventually, Gina was going to run off with one of her clients and elope in Croatia, leaving me to figure out life on my own as a lonely, unemployed homeless person who wouldn't even be able to make street friends all that easily? I mean, I wasn't *not* worried about it.

Gina didn't let it go. "Have some fun. Enjoy yourself. You've been too focused on your job hunt."

"Because I need a job," I said before clarifying, "A real job."

"The jobs will be there," said Brent, who had a very well-paying job from what I understood.

"I think what Brent is trying to say is that one or two or twelve dates aren't going to cause your job applications to be deleted," said Gina.

She had a point.

I shrugged, looking between Gina and the rest of my well-meaning, slightly red-cheeked friends. "All right."

Her eyes expanded in almost shock.

There was a whoop from a few of our other friends around us, already naming people they had in mind or crossing them off their mental lists after they already got married or were in long-term relationships.

"This is much more fun than doing a Secret Santa," someone said in the group.

"For real? We're doing this?" Gina asked one last time to give me an out. She raised her eyebrows imploringly.

I let the moment sit between us all as they waited for my answer.

I nodded.

Brent nudged his mug against mine. They clunked together, and a few drops fell over the edge and on my jeans. "Cheers to that."

two

I COULD TELL I was going to have a massive hangover in the morning. Rolling off the side of my bed, I woke up before the sun, unable to ignore the dryness in my throat. I might've still been a little tipsy, not bothering to pull on my sweatpants before I lumbered toward the kitchen.

A few of the lamps were still on, glowing through the small apartment as I reached up toward one of the last pint glasses that was from my alma mater, red and gold letters faded from going through the dishwasher so many times. I watched the water run from the sink faucet before I dipped the glass underneath, letting it fill until the very top.

Leaning over the sink, I ducked my head under the faucet in a very unladylike fashion that was only more hilarious, considering I hadn't put on any pants before I slid out of bed. Hydration was paramount when it was clear that I could be dying from lack of water, and I might've still be a little drunk.

I slurped a sip just as I heard the door shut behind me. I chuckled, water dripping down my chin as I turned around to see a similarly disheveled Gina likely walking to stick her head under the faucet with me.

Only it wasn't Gina.

I gasped, stepping back to run into the sink.

Josh stood in front of me. His hand extended, as if he would attempt to catch me before I made an even bigger fool of myself. "Sorry, I didn't mean to scare you. I was just getting in."

"It's, um ..." I cleared my throat.

Wiping my damp mouth off with the back of my hand, I set my glass down on the counter. Or at least, I attempted to.

There were a lot of dirty glasses in the way, sounding like a small catastrophe of noise.

I cringed.

Yep. My head was going to hurt in the morning, wasn't it?

Note to self: never let Gina play bartender ever again.

I focused back on Josh, who was watching my clumsiness.

"It's fine. I was just getting water. Your sister made some kind of espresso–pumpkin vodka combination that might have scarred me for life."

He cleared his throat, but didn't take his eyes off me. He didn't move at all. "That sounds like her. Water is probably the best choice."

"I, um, thought so too."

Turning around, I turned the tap back on and waited a moment for the water to cool. Once it did, I refilled the glass and turned back to Josh. He was still standing there, though he'd moved to take off his coat.

It was only then that I realized I still wasn't wearing pants and Josh was getting a whole lot of light-blue cotton panty action right now.

I blushed, trying to cover it with a long sip of water, which felt like heaven. I struggled not to inhale the entire glass, almost gasping by the time I came back up. "Mmm, yum."

"You should probably refill again before you head to bed. Gina never hesitates to give anyone a hangover."

I filled the glass back up. "I should be good now."

"Sounds like you had a good night."

"We did. I hope you did too." I waved a hand at him in his jeans and pressed shirt.

Somehow, since the last time I had seen Josh, he'd gotten a new style, as well as a personality transplant, different from the guy I remembered who was constantly in his frat-boy business-casual tops.

"Wherever you were tonight. In the big city. Living it up and enjoying yourself—" I cut myself off like I should've cut myself off the pumpkin salted-caramel mess long before I did. "Sorry. I'm going to bed."

He gave a small, tight nod.

"Night," I said before quickly retreating toward my room.

After a second, as I started to shut the door, I heard him whisper. "Night, Bri."

three

I GUESS TRUSTING my friends with my love life was how I had gotten to this point, sitting at a table and checking my watch again to make sure I had the time right.

Fifteen minutes late.

So far, I was really starting my twelve blind dates before Christmas—when I was set to go home with Gina to where we had grown up—with a bang.

And this one wasn't even an actual date.

It was a practice date with Gina. Though it wasn't out of character for her to be running fashionably late, I was feeling more than a little frustrated with her at this point. I could be home right now, being productive.

Or at least, I could be home with a late-night tea, attempting to be productive before turning on another episode of a reality dating television.

There was one show right now about finding a last-minute date before the holidays. It felt a little too pertinent to my own love life, but at least I wasn't broadcasting it.

It was nicer to make fun of others attempting to find love rather than recognize that you had basically been set up on your own version of embarrassing relationship challenges by somewhat friends, who stood you up.

I sighed, wondering how bad it would be if I checked my email another time. I had a good feeling about that last job that I'd applied for yesterday. It was a staff writing position at a small art magazine that usually posted online and through a quarterly publication about local hot spots. They just had to reach back out to me. Other than the fact that I was new to the area and still hadn't explored farther than my own neighborhood block, I was perfect for it.

Or I hoped it was.

I opened my phone and texted Gina.

> Where are you???

No response.

There wasn't even a tiny *Read* check mark that told me she'd glanced at it.

Unlike me, Gina had come alive since we'd moved to the city. I wasn't naive enough to think things would go back to the way they had been in high school—when we spent entire summers in each other's bedroom, daydreaming about living in New York and having grown-up jobs and grown-up apartments. We'd grown separately for almost half a decade, and now ... well, we were still best friends. But we were trying to figure out how these slightly newer, more independent versions of ourselves fit together again.

Some days, when it was just us in our cramped apartment, eating bodega ramen and laughing about the guy upstairs who rollerbladed at midnight, it was like no time had passed. But then there were weekends, when she slipped on her slim black gallery dress and left for openings, full of wine and collectors and people who talked in breathy tones about "negative space," and I felt a little unmoored. Waiting to be pulled into the current again. Waiting for Gina to lead, like she used to.

Once, as she'd lined her eyes with a precision I could never match, she'd glanced over at me from the mirror and said, "You should come sometime. To one of the gallery things. Think of the story you could write. Beef up your portfolio a little. You could even meet people. I could help you design a business card even."

"For what business?" I'd asked.

But she'd had a point.

My portfolio was … fine. Mostly padded with college newspaper clippings and the rare personal essay I had managed to get published on niche online sites that paid in "exposure" and vague compliments. A glittery gallery profile might give it the shine it needed.

Still, instead of getting dressed, I tapped open my email. Again.

Nothing. Not even a polite rejection today—just the usual promotions about going back to school to pursue a new online degree.

What liars.

Been there, done that. And all I had to show for it was an expensive piece of paper, folded neatly into my Important Documents folder, buried beneath expired leases and an emergency contact form from a job I hadn't even gotten.

I checked the time. I would give Gina two more minutes. Maybe three. Then I was leaving.

The server—some poor guy with boy-band bangs and the awkward energy of someone who felt obligated to care—kept glancing my way like he wasn't sure if he should offer me water or emotional support.

Eventually, he made his way over. "Hi there."

I smiled.

"Are you still waiting for someone?"

We both looked at the empty chair across from me, the full glass of untouched water, the ring of condensation slowly bleeding into the red tablecloth.

"I don't think I am," I said, offering another tight smile. "But I figured I'd give them another minute."

"Would you like a drink or anything while you wait?"

I opened my mouth. "No, I'm—"

"I'd *love* a drink, thank you," came a voice that wasn't mine. Deeper. Confident. Familiar.

I blinked.

Across from me, a tall form slid into the chair. It definitely was not Gina's petite frame. But there was something familiar in the tight curls, the smirk.

Josh.

Gina's older brother—the walking contradiction of charming grifter and accidental philosopher we thought he'd become over the past few years. He had Gina's hair, but none of her restraint when it was called for.

The server, unfazed, whipped a small, laminated menu out of his apron like he was used to odd entrances.

Josh's grin widened like he'd just been handed a prize. "Ah, thanks. Do you guys have any of those ridiculous holiday drinks happening yet?"

The server didn't blink. Just handed him another slimmer menu with a practiced nod.

Josh scanned the list with exaggerated focus. "Let's see ... we've got a Jingle Bell Martini, a Snowy White Russian ..." He looked up at me and raised an eyebrow. "Have you ever tried a Cinnamon Sleigh Ride?"

"I don't think I'm the target audience."

"That's exactly why it's brilliant."

I stared at him, still trying to figure out what exactly was happening here even though it was clear. Gina had put him up to this, hadn't she?

"I'll have the Red-Hot Santa-tini. Or is it *Santini*?"

"Either works." The server suppressed a smile before he turned to me, pen still poised. "Would you like anything?"

"Oh, I, uh ..."

"Go on. Get something," encouraged Josh with a sharp nod, pivoting the holiday menu toward me.

God, they really were absurd holiday drinks.

"I'll have the Pomegranate Spritz," I ordered. It sounded like the most normal option, listed in swirling font.

"I'll be right back with those."

He smiled casually, like showing up in his sister's place on my first blind-date practice run was a totally normal thing. "Hey."

"Hi," I replied.

Without missing a beat, Josh shrugged off his coat and settled into the seat across from me like he did this sort of thing all the time.

"What are you doing?" I asked, blinking at him.

"Taking off my jacket," he said, glancing down as if to double-check that, yes, that was indeed the action he'd just performed.

"No, I mean, what are you doing here?" I clarified, trying not to sound like I was panicking.

"Gina got caught up."

My phone buzzed before I could ask what that even meant. I grabbed it like it might hold the answers to the universe.

> Sending my bro to meet you. I'm so, SO SORRY. Big work things are happening! I can't wait to tell you about everything. Don't be mad.

I looked up slowly from Gina's message, trying to process the fact that my best friend had officially lost her mind.

Josh sat there like this was the most natural thing in the world, completely unbothered, taking in the mismatched chairs and fairy lights strung across the ceiling. He didn't even look guilty.

Why Josh? She was supposed to meet me. She knew this was a trial run, a warm-up before the real blind dates began. Why would she send her brother instead?

> Not mad. He's here. But a bit of notice would have been nice.

> It's better anyway. You should practice with a guy before the real thing. Also, you and Josh are making the apartment weird.

Great. So, she'd noticed.

The weirdness between Josh and me had reached observable levels. It looked like she'd decided to fix it in the most chaotic way possible. I hadn't thought Gina had a passive-aggressive bone in her body. Guess I was wrong.

But Josh was helping with rent.

The rent. The very wonderful, no longer full-priced rent.

If I repeated it enough times, maybe I wouldn't freak out.

I exhaled, letting go of the text exchange and turning my focus back to the tall, just barely disheveled man across from me. He was inspecting the quirky, over-the-top restaurant decor like it was a museum exhibit. Like he had all the time in the world.

Stop. Stop it.

He noticed me watching and flashed another grin.

Since when did he smile so much?

"So," he said, "I'm your practice date?"

"Apparently."

"I figured you'd be out or working tonight," I said, trying not to sound like I'd spent the day rehearsing real conversations for someone who was not him.

"Nope. Open schedule," he said, then went on, "Been exploring a bit. Seeing friends. It's been nice actually—just … staying still for a while."

I tilted my head. "Since … two years ago?"

His smile faded just slightly, settling into something softer. "About, yeah."

The server reappeared with our drinks, setting mine—a fruity something in a wide wineglass—in front of me. But Josh's? His looked like it belonged in a sci-fi cocktail competition.

It arrived in a martini glass with a rim of cinnamon sugar. The server grinned as he pulled out what looked suspiciously like a fancy water gun. With a press of the trigger, a shimmering bubble floated out and landed perfectly atop Josh's drink.

All the nearby tables turned to stare at the performance we'd ordered.

Josh watched the spectacle with boyish delight. Then, without hesitation, he poked the bubble, and it collapsed in a puff of cranberry-scented smoke.

"Whoa," he said, grinning at the server. "That's awesome. Thanks."

"Enjoy," the server said, vanishing like a magician after a trick.

I stared at the glass, equal parts impressed and confused. "Wow. That was … something."

Josh raised his glass. "To practice."

I hesitated for a beat, then clinked mine against his.

He reached to take a sip. Pouting his plush bottom lip, he

managed to look a little stunned. "And it doesn't taste nearly as much like cough medicine as I imagined."

"If you thought it was going to taste like cough medicine, why did you order it?"

"I like to try new things," he said. "Life is too short not to have a little fun."

I reached to try my own drink. It wasn't too bad either. "Even when it comes to crazy holiday drinks?"

"Especially then," said Josh. "Low risk, high reward. Well, some of the time, there's a high reward. If not, at least now I can say that I've had a martini with a show."

That was something he definitely *could* say. However, I wasn't sure that I ever thought he would.

I kind of forgot just how carefree Josh was. Or at least, he used to be on special occasions when we were young. As Gina's older brother, he always felt a lot older than us—until he wasn't so much anymore. Most of the time, he hung out with his friends outside of their house, where it was basically *the place* to be growing up.

Josh and Gina's mom was the perfect sort of mom. She cared when you spoke and genuinely asked how your day was when you arrived from school, never bothered by where you dropped your backpack. She always made the best snacks she'd lay out, "just in case you're a bit peckish," and never minded when I ended up staying for dinner—or well past dinner.

I often didn't want to go home to where I was living with my grandmother before she passed away my senior year. After that, I was eighteen, and no one else seemed to question how I was doing on my own. The small two-bedroom single-story house that hadn't been updated since it had been built in the '50s, however, was quiet. Too quiet.

"You never said where you got your job since you moved here," I said, trying to keep Josh talking so that I didn't go through all my past memories of the town and house that paid for my tuition, though not much else in the condition it was in.

His forehead creased. "I didn't?"

Maybe Gina was right in the fact that I had been acting weird around the house. Sure, Josh wasn't there all the time, but when he was, I hid in my room and only came out for water and the few snacks I stashed in the back of the cabinet.

"I got a job back in IT."

"Big, fancy start-up work again?" I kind of thought when he had dropped off the face of the earth two years ago that he was done with all that, though it made sense. It was what he had gone to school for, and he clearly was good at it. "I thought you were over all that."

"Oh, I am. I don't think you could pay me to go back to another tech start-up or whatever again." He chuckled. "Nah, done with killing myself to not even live. You don't need to, and in the end, I didn't care all that much about what I was even doing. Not like some of the guys I'm still friends with who are there. Anyway, I got a good gig working in a middle school a few weeks ago."

"You're kidding."

"Nope. The technology called to me once more, and I answered. It is just in a different, less *I want to gouge my eyes out so I never have to look at a screen ever again* kind of way. I've been working at the school for the past few weeks, drinking all the coffee I want from the teachers' lounge and plugging in computer chargers for technologically challenged almost retirees."

"Wow. Sounds like you're loving it."

"You know what?" He looked like he really considered that. "I think I am. Or at least liking it enough, which I'll take."

"I didn't think you'd come back," I said quietly.

Josh looked up. "What do you mean?"

"To the city. Home." I shrugged, offering both options like one might feel safer than the other. "You seemed like you were doing fine out there—traveling, living your life ... with everyone else you were traveling with."

I took another sip of my sangria, letting the warmth of the brandy smooth out the edge in my voice. Hopefully, it masked the fact that I'd seen nearly every photo he'd posted over the last two years—sparingly, yes, but enough to remind me that he was still out there, still moving. Still not here.

"I did enjoy it," he said after a beat, his tone gentler than I'd expected. "A lot actually. Turns out, there's a whole world to see when you let yourself look."

He gave a half laugh. "Pretty sure my bank called twice just to check that I wasn't having a midlife crisis. Quarter-life?"

"Were you?"

He grinned. "Honestly? Probably. But I think it worked. Got just enough vacation time banked from that 'big, fancy corporate' job—your words, by the way. Figured I should use it while I still had it. Life's short, you know?"

"So you said," I murmured, not trusting myself to say more.

Josh leaned back slightly, his fingers toying with the corner of the menu. "But, yeah, I'm back now. Zipper on my suitcase finally gave out. I took it as a sign. Sorry. I'm rambling."

"I don't mind," I said before I could stop myself.

And I didn't. Not even a little. Which was a problem.

This was supposed to be a fake date. A practice date. A warm-up round before the real thing. But sitting across from Josh, listening to his voice, watching the way he smiled a little when he talked about the world—this wasn't practice. This was the thing I'd been trying to avoid.

Because talking to Josh? It was ... nice.

Too nice.

And that was exactly what I didn't want to admit.

Ever since Gina and I had moved into the apartment, we'd been bumping into people from the old days—faces from high school, college, the ones who'd drifted to the city like we had. It was strange and oddly comforting.

But Josh?

Josh was different.

He was the kind of familiar that made my chest ache in that low, quiet way you couldn't quite explain. The kind of familiar that reminded me of how he used to be. And how everything had changed after the accident. How he vanished, leaving nothing but an empty room and a trail of stories that sounded more like myths than memories.

For a long time, I figured I'd never see him again. I'd pictured him settling down somewhere far away with a sun-kissed partner who spoke seven languages and wore linen without wrinkles. They'd raise brilliant, nomadic little children and drink espresso at three p.m. and make the rest of us look like we were stuck in slow motion.

But now he was here. He was sitting across from me like it was nothing. Like we hadn't left things unsaid.

Maybe he had moved on. Maybe he didn't even remember how humiliating that night had been for me.

Unfortunately, I still did.

Josh glanced back down at the menu, his brow furrowing slightly before he glanced up at me with a spark of amusement. "Did you pick this place?"

I shook my head.

"Gina," we said at the same time.

We both looked around, taking in the tiny plates and elaborately described appetizers. I scanned the menu again, landing on something I couldn't pronounce.

"Who names a dish *bouchée à la reine*?" I asked under my breath. "Sounds like a dare."

Josh laughed. "I think it's French for *you're not getting full tonight.*"

I smiled despite myself. And just like that, the weirdness thinned out. A little.

"Do you want to finish this drink and go somewhere else?" asked Josh.

My forehead creased, though he was already taking another long sip of his cheery drink until there was nothing but a final few drips sitting at the bottom.

"We really don't have to go anywhere else. I'm happy to call it and head home to eat one of my microwavable noodle dinners really."

That sounded sad, didn't it? Certainly not what a normal girl would admit to and certainly not on a date, fake or not. But this wasn't a date.

This was me. And this was Josh.

And we would never be on a date.

Ha! The hilarity of that.

I pushed a smile to make myself believe it even more and hoped that it sold my complete unperturbed-ness of how this evening had taken a turn from a girls' night out with Gina.

"What? Why not?" he asked.

"Because," I said. He waited for more. "You really don't have to be here or keep doing this. It was supposed to be my pretend practice date, and I get that you are doing something nice for your sister when she called, but ..."

"I'm nothing but dedicated to the cause," he said seriously.

I raised an eyebrow.

"Impressive," he commented, reaching up to push up his own eyebrow. Whenever he let go, it fell. "I could never get that right."

I shrugged. "Party trick."

"Anyway"—he took a deep breath, as if coming up with

some sort of way to say what he was about to say—"what I'm really trying to say is that there's a hockey game on. I know a bar just down the street. It could be a fun time. Do you really want this to be the end of your night?"

Josh already passed the server his card effortlessly as he passed by. I tried to reach out to offer to split our check of what was likely overpriced holiday drinks, but it was too late.

"You in?"

I glanced down at my lifeless phone again on the edge of the table.

No notifications. No emails. Yet I should really get back home. Get back on the hunt. Work on the freelance projects that needed to be done sooner than later so that, hopefully, I'd attract new clients.

My stomach growled.

Josh grinned as if my body had answered for me. "Pretty please? Come on. You know it's my treat. And I can't stand to let my little sister down."

Is that who he couldn't stand to let down?

"Think of it as a thank-you for letting me crash on your couch for the last month." He stood up as he pulled on his coat, waiting for me to do the same. The server came back with the check, and he signed off without glancing at it. "They have fantastic wings. Better than baked artichoke cream bruschetta. Actually, maybe my sister has a point; that sounds amazing. But still, you want to mix up your boring practice date to a night you might actually enjoy?"

He reached for my coat on the back of my seat and extended it to me with raised eyebrows and waited. "You only live once, remember?"

four

"YOU ONLY LIVE ONCE."

It was something about what Josh had said—"Life's short"
—that hit me in a strangely familiar way. Not just because it
was true, but because I'd heard it before.

It sounded almost exactly like the motto I had given myself
when I left the suburbs for the first time at nineteen, dragging a
rolling suitcase, stuffed with too many pairs of plaid pajama
pants and three different holiday sweaters I couldn't bear to
leave behind. I was determined to make the most of everything.

To say yes. To show up in a way I hadn't all throughout high
school or before that, when I was just trying to make it by.

Although, if I was being honest, I thought Gina had said it
first.

She was always ahead of the times.

She was also the one who had guilt-tripped me into coming
back home with her for Christmas during our first year of
college, even though I'd been looking forward to having the
shared dorm room all to myself. I had planned on a quiet week
with bad TV, stolen cafeteria snacks, and finally catching up on
sleep.

But then Gina had called, laying it on thick in a way that she knew would get to me.

"My mom's making her homemade peppermint bark. You know, the peppermint bark. The one you single-handedly ate an entire tin of?"

That was the bait.

Then came the guilt.

"You're basically the more emotionally stable daughter my mom wishes she had. Are you seriously going to rob her of that joy?"

I should've. I really, really should've.

Because when I showed up on the Huttons' doorstep, trailing behind Gina with a weekend bag slung over my shoulder, the wide-eyed surprise on Mrs. Hutton's face told me everything I needed to know.

No one had told her I was coming.

"I wanted it to be a surprise!" Gina squealed when I shot her a look sharp enough to cut tinsel.

Her mom recovered quickly though, pulling me into a warm hug that smelled like cinnamon and confidence. "Brielle, sweetheart! You're here!"

Her dad barely looked up from the newspaper, but he nodded once. "Good to see you, Brielle," he said in that calm, always-unbothered way of his that made it feel like I'd never left.

Once I was inside, the house fell into that familiar rhythm. Gina caught everyone up on school gossip while I helped her mom ice sugar cookies in the kitchen, careful to make mine look better than Gina's just to annoy her.

Mrs. Hutton asked about my classes and whether I'd picked a major. I told her I was still committed to English.

"But you don't want to be a teacher?" she asked, tilting her head. She passed me the bowl of frosting.

I shook my head. "Not in the slightest."

"Huh," she said, as if she couldn't quite compute that.

It seemed like a common response I was slowly getting used to.

Later that evening, we curled up on the couch to watch a Christmas movie. It was one of those older ones, where the characters rediscover the "true meaning" of the holidays, which always boiled down to some combination of family, forgiveness, and falling in love under twinkle lights.

I was halfway through a mug of hot cocoa when the front door blew open and the film was immediately paused.

A gust of freezing winter air swept through the house. Two men stepped inside, wrapped in dark coats and layers, boots thudding on the tiles.

I didn't need to see their faces to know one of them was Josh.

Dropping the bags, Josh yanked his beanie off the top of his head. His puff of hair was slightly longer than the last time I had seen him when he was home this past summer.

"Ah, they made it!" Mrs. Hutton stood from the couch and raced over to them. "Oh goodness, so glad you guys got in before the storm."

"There's a storm?"

The second gust of wind, sending the door slamming behind them and sealing us off from the heavy snowstorm, was enough for Mrs. Hutton to cock her head to the side sarcastically.

"Just a small one." She wrapped her arms around her son before looking behind him toward the second person in tow. "I thought you were bringing Lauren."

Josh shook his head, lips pressed together in answer. He

wrapped an arm around his friend I recognized from when he had brought him back home last year and the year prior for Thanksgiving and once during summer break when we all went to the beach. "I brought Nick. Don't make him feel bad."

"I already have a complex," Nick joked. "Nice to see you, Mrs. Hutton."

Mrs. Hutton welcomed them inside, similar to how they had welcomed me and Gina, with a gentle hug and directions on where to put their duffel bags and loads of laundry he had also brought home with him. "It's so good to see you both."

The couch was full, as Gina was passed out with her head lolling over the arm.

Looking for a seat, Josh's eyes flicked around the room before landing on me. He cleared his throat and gave the smallest of shrugs before sinking down onto the couch beside me.

"Hey, Bri. Long time no see."

"Merry Christmas, Josh."

"Merry Christmas," he echoed, the corner of his mouth tugging up.

Conversation picked up again as if no time had passed. The parents asked about the drive, finals, and how they were adjusting to life after fall semester. It was just as they had been with Gina earlier. Josh, in typical fashion, relayed the events of the last few weeks with exaggerated flair, tossing in jokes that made his dad chuckle under his breath and his mom swat at his knee with a playful, "Joshua."

Nick chimed in now and then with quieter updates, but eventually excused himself, muttering something about an early morning.

As the room settled into a quieter rhythm, Gina stirred beside me, rubbing her eyes. "Bed?"

We said good night to everyone before heading upstairs.

"Sorry about that," she murmured as we reached the bathroom.

"About what?"

"My brother."

I frowned, toothbrush halfway to my mouth. "What's wrong with your brother?"

She gave me a look. "You know. Just ... him. Bursting in like a hurricane. Classic Josh."

"Says the dramatic art student," I teased.

She grinned and bumped her hip into mine. "Hey."

We brushed our teeth side by side, the way we had at every sleepover since we were twelve, and crawled into the bed we used to pile into with popcorn bowls and high-school crushes on our minds. The lights clicked off. Gina fell asleep within minutes, her breathing evening out.

I lay there, the blanket tucked under my chin, staring into the dark.

The house had gone mostly still—save for the faint murmur of voices and the creaking of stairs as everyone slowly made their way to bed. I kept my eyes shut, willing sleep to take me, but it didn't.

It never did when my thoughts got like this. Restless. Wandering.

Thirty minutes passed. Then an hour.

Quietly, I slipped from the bed, pulled on thick socks, and crept down the stairs.

The kitchen was unchanged—just as I remembered it. But somehow, after only a few months away, everything felt older. Smaller. The ghosts of past holidays still hung in the corners, in the way the chairs creaked and the thermostat buzzed.

I filled a glass of water and paced slowly, back and forth on the cold tiles. I didn't realize how much time I'd spent in this house over the years—escaping my own mostly. Back when my grandmother still sort of recognized me and then later, after the house fell into silence altogether.

I hadn't just been Gina's friend. I'd been the stray they let stay.

A soft flicker of light caught my eye from the living room.

Still up, Mr. H?

I shuffled closer and peeked around the corner. I stopped.

Not Mr. H.

Josh was stretched out on the couch, resting against a pile of mismatched throw pillows. An animated movie played on the screen, something I vaguely recognized from childhood. He looked ... different like this.

Softer. Calmer. Or maybe just less guarded.

"Are you okay?" he asked, his voice low, not startled.

I blinked, caught. "I just came down for some water," I said, holding up my glass as proof.

He nodded, his eyes returning briefly to the screen. "Can't sleep?"

"Not really."

"Yeah," he said, rubbing the back of his neck. "It's been evading me lately."

His gaze flicked back to me, pausing just a second too long on my ridiculous pajama pants—the candy-cane ones that were way too long and puddled around my ankles. Still, he didn't say anything.

"If you want to sit ..." he offered, patting the spot beside him. "It's not like I'm going anywhere."

I hesitated, then stepped forward and lowered myself onto the couch.

For years, I'd dreaded moments like this—just me and Josh in a room. My heart used to thud like a bass drum in my chest. My hands would get clammy, and I'd develop this terrible habit of licking my lips over and over again until they felt raw. It was like a reflex I couldn't stop—some weird way to keep myself from blurting out, *You're the coolest person I've ever met, and I think about you way too often.*

But we hadn't done much talking back then. Mostly orbiting. Avoiding. Pretending not to notice the weird electricity whenever we did make eye contact for longer than five seconds. Even if I was the only one who must've felt it.

In spite of that, Josh was the one who had talked me off the ledge when I nearly bailed on going out of state for college.

Gina had been at rehearsal, and I was sitting on their front steps, trying not to cry. Josh came home from school early, found me there, and stayed.

He didn't say much. But what he did say stuck.

"I get why you're scared," he'd said. *"But you don't get to stay small just because it's comfortable. You'll regret it."*

And he had been right.

He always had this way of saying things like that—like they weren't a big deal, like he wasn't changing my life slowly, permanently.

I had gone to college out of state, and the first few months were a transition, but one I could handle, even if my one grammar class kicked me in the butt more than any English class in my life and made me question the decision more than a few times.

Because I often asked, *What if I fail?*

But then I heard Josh's words and thought, *What if I don't?*

And now, here we were sitting next to each other once again in the dark of the Hutton household.

"How are you doing?" I asked as I fought to get comfortable next to him. "Final year of college. That's exciting."

"I'm doing good."

"Figuring out what you are doing after graduation?"

"As much as I can," he said.

He didn't seem as thrilled as I'd figured he would be. As much as he had been when he first invited me even to sit on the couch with him.

"Yep. It's great," he said.

"You sure?"

"Positive," he said, though blandly.

"You just seem different."

He stared at me. "Maybe that's just you."

I shrugged, not commenting on that. Since I'd started college, I'd felt different, but we weren't talking about me. "Are you upset then?"

"Upset?"

"About ... Lauren."

His eyebrows bent low over his gaze.

"I just thought ... she didn't come, and your mom said that you were bringing a girlfriend that you'd been with. I thought it was kind of serious."

"My mom likes to get ahead of herself," he said swiftly. "I'm surprised you are here though this year."

"What do you mean?" Did he not want to see me?

I shifted on the couch to get ready to head back to bed. I'd likely already overstayed my welcome here. It was his house after all. I was the guest.

"Surprised that you don't have a boyfriend by now or someone from school who invited you home with them for the holiday."

"Nope. No one is interested in me like that."

"I highly doubt that."

"Then I guess you'll have to conduct a survey," I challenged.

He sighed, glancing at me again. "It's good to see you. I mean, it's good to see everyone here."

"I thought you came back for Thanksgiving."

"I did. I just mean … I'm used to you here—with my sister. So, it's good. Like everyone is here."

"Yeah, I'm … I'm glad to be here too," I said, relaxing further into the cushions.

I must've been more tired than I realized as the movie went on.

* * *

Blinking my eyes open, it took me a second to realize where I was. I wasn't back at school or in Gina's bed. I tried to sit up, but was quickly halted. "Oh."

His hand held me against his chest. "You're fine."

"Sorry," I said.

All around me was warm. The blankets from over the top of the couch had been draped over top of my body and, in relation, Josh's. And I had fallen asleep on Josh's chest. His arms cradled around me, keeping us in place as I arched my neck back to see his dark lashes softly blink against his cheeks.

"I didn't mean to fall asleep."

"I fell asleep too," he said, and I could hear the slight scratchiness to his voice. His hand, too, kept me in place before his thumb started to stroke back and forth on my upper arm.

I couldn't help myself as I let my eyes slip closed before popping right back open, trying to stay awake while relishing in the feeling. Josh was holding me, and I fit perfectly into the curve of his shoulder.

"It's all right."

"I should go back upstairs," I said, but didn't move.

"Don't you want to go back and find out how the movie ends?"

I stared at him for a second before I nodded. "Yeah, okay."

"I won't let you fall asleep this time."

* * *

The thing about the Hutton house, being the one all the friends filtered through, was that games were inevitable. And once cheap alcohol entered the mix, it became a free-for-all of nostalgia-fueled competitiveness.

Gina had the brilliant idea of throwing a holiday party at home while her parents were down the block at their own gathering. The plan? Re-create childhood chaos, but with more wine and fewer broken bones. Though, honestly, the way everyone was moving through the house, it didn't feel that far off from the old days. Sleepovers, tree climbing, and that one infamous game of manhunt that had earned Nick a cast and a lifetime of glory.

We'd already played a chaotic round of charades and half watched a holiday movie before someone inevitably suggested hide-and-seek. It was an old favorite. Everyone grabbed a partner without hesitation—except Gina. She latched on to the nearest person, and it wasn't me.

Before I could even blink, Josh was at my side.

"Come on," he muttered, grabbing my hand and tugging me along. "Clock's ticking."

He didn't wait for a response—he never did, not when his competitive streak kicked in. I remembered it well. Apparently, it hadn't dulled over the years, and if I was honest, being around him brought out a streak of my own. All night, we'd challenged each other. A rematch at tipsy checkers. Charades so intense that Gina nearly choked while laughing. And now this.

He pulled me into the laundry room, both of us laughing as he shut the door quietly behind us. The warmth from the dryer and the buzz of peppermint schnapps made everything feel electric.

"Shh," Josh warned with a grin. One hand held my arm as

he tried to wedge us deeper into the narrow corner. "You're not going to make me lose this."

He pushed me back gently, his hand brushing over my stomach as he tried to make space. It was cramped. Close. But somehow, it didn't feel uncomfortable.

It felt like ... we fit.

Like puzzle pieces.

His body pressed into mine, solid and warm, and the room suddenly felt very still. His hand moved slowly, carefully up from my waist, skimming over my chest and brushing the side of my neck.

My breath caught.

So did his.

When our eyes met, something shifted. Or maybe it had been shifting all night, quietly building between laughter and shared glances and late-night conversations after everyone else had gone to bed.

I wasn't imagining this.

Josh was going to kiss me.

This was actually happening. I could feel it in the way his chest rose and fell against mine, in how his gaze dropped to my lips and lingered. The room spun slightly, or maybe that was just me. I leaned forward.

"Wh-what are you doing?" he asked, voice barely above a whisper.

I froze, eyes wide. My heart slammed against my ribs.

What was I doing?

I whispered, "I ... I was going to kiss you."

It was the truth. The bravest, most terrifying truth I'd likely ever spoken. I could've brushed it off, but I didn't. I was about to kiss Josh Hutton, and he ...

Josh's expression shifted, eyes narrowing slightly, as if he hadn't expected me to admit it. "Kiss me?"

"I thought ... when you led me in here and then how you looked at me ..."

"How I looked at you?"

"I'm sorry. I thought you were going to kiss me."

"You thought I was going to kiss you?" His tone wasn't unkind exactly. But it wasn't encouraging either. It was laced with caution. Like he was trying to backpedal through fog.

"Yes." Heat rose in my cheeks. "I thought ... after this week, after everything ... I thought maybe you felt something too. I thought we were ..."

"Having fun," he said, cutting in. "We're literally playing a game right now."

The words sliced through me. So stark. So final.

I blinked, trying to keep my expression neutral. I could feel the tightening in my chest, the way my throat was beginning to close. "Right. Sure. Fun."

"I mean ..." He hesitated, eyes still on me, but now unreadable. "I'm definitely not going to kiss my little sister's kid best friend."

I stiffened. "I'm not a kid."

"The fact that you feel the need to say that kind of proves my point."

My breath left me in a rush. I stepped back—or tried to, but there was nowhere to go in the tiny space. I pushed gently against his chest until he moved, just far enough to give me room to breathe.

"You were the one who said it," I muttered, not looking at him.

"I chose to be your partner because I felt bad for you," he said quietly, like it was something that should make this better. "You said it yourself. You don't have anyone here except Gina. No friends at school. I just didn't want you to feel left out."

I stared at him, cold settling into my bones. "You felt bad for me?"

He felt bad for me.

"No one else picked you. I thought I was doing something good. I was doing a decent thing. The decent thing."

My lips parted, but no words came out.

Because what did you even say to that?

The room was still warm. The dryer still hummed. But all I could feel was the sharp sting of embarrassment crawling over my skin.

So, that was it. The moment I'd waited for, dreamed about, built up in my head for years. It hadn't been something. It had been pity.

Pity!

It stung more than if he'd just laughed in my face.

I struggled to swallow as the heavy burn of emotion started to crawl its way up my throat.

No one else had even known that I was coming to Christmas until I showed up. In Gina's words, it was for a surprise. In my world, it was because I was forgotten and likely more unwanted than wanted.

Again.

"I didn't even want to ..." He drifted off. "Fuck. I didn't want ..."

He was lying.

He had to be.

Somewhere deep inside, I knew it. I knew that no one could look at me the way he just had, touch me the way he had, without some kind of feeling. He had been leaning in. His hand had moved to my neck. He was teasing, laughing, looking at me like—

No. He was just messing with me. That had to be it.

Except another voice—a quieter, meaner one—whispered something else entirely.

Of course he didn't like me.

I was younger.

A kid.

Some desperate little loser who had mistaken five minutes of closeness for affection.

I felt sick. My mouth was dry, my cheeks hot with humiliation I couldn't scrub off. I couldn't even look at him as he turned, shoved open the laundry room door, and disappeared.

He got found five minutes later. One of the first people out.

I stayed.

Tucked behind the dryer, knees drawn up to my chest, I waited in silence for nearly half an hour. I "won" the game. But I'd never felt more like a loser in my entire life.

By the time I wandered back out, Gina was already scanning the room for me. She spotted my face and pounced.

"Why are you a sourpuss?"

"I'm not."

She narrowed her eyes. "Your hair's a mess. Oh my God. Did you hook up with someone while hiding? Is that how you lasted so long? You have to tell me who."

She grabbed my hands like she could pull the answer from my palms, then dropped them with an actual gasp. "It was Nick, wasn't it? Nick found you. Ew. Oh my God, it was Nick."

Her face scrunched up in theatrical disgust. "Nope. I don't even want to know. If it's someone vaguely related to my brother, I'm opting out. I've already reached my lifetime quota of Josh-adjacent nonsense."

"It wasn't Nick," I said, my voice flat.

She studied me for a second longer, then shrugged. "All right. I believe you."

"Thanks."

"But you could tell me. You know that, right?"

"I know. Nothing happened. I'm just tired."

"Promise?"

That, at least, was easy. "Promise."

"And you promise nothing will ever happen with, like, anyone even orbiting my brother's weird, womanizer, back-packing-around-Europe-for-enlightenment vibe?"

My heart stuttered. I raised my eyebrows in mock offense.

"I already have enough Josh in my life," she muttered. "I don't need you becoming my honorary sister-in-law to some douche canoe he dragged home from a yoga retreat in Costa Rica."

"Nothing will ever happen," I said. "Ever."

"Good. Because gag. Right?"

Right.

That night, we all went to bed. Gina passed out almost immediately. I lay there, staring at the ceiling, twisting the blankets in my fists, listening to the faint murmur of the television downstairs.

Josh was probably still down there—half watching another movie, stretched out on the couch like nothing had happened. Like I hadn't tried to kiss him. Like I hadn't told him the truth.

I thought about sneaking down and asking him what his deal was. I wanted to. But what I really wanted was to go back in time—to two nights ago, when I hadn't said anything, hadn't tried, hadn't made a fool of myself in a cramped laundry room with someone who would never look at me the way I looked at him.

This is better, I told myself.

Josh? He dated girls who wore matching pajama sets and made vision boards. Girls who wanted to be teachers or lawyers. Girls who volunteered at shelters or had been to Greece on mission trips.

Not girls like me.

Not Brielle, who was known mostly for being the smart one. The decent writer. The overachiever. The girl who read quietly in the back seat while everyone else paired off at high-school dances.

I was proud of all that. I was. I was building something real for myself. Bigger than crushes.

Bigger than this moment.

So, what was I thinking?

How could I ever think that Josh Hutton would ever like me?

five

IT HAD BEEN YEARS. Years.

Yet the moment Josh held the door to the bar open for me like some kind of rom-com gentleman, the weight of that laundry room crushed me all over again.

I stepped inside anyway, chin up, shoulders squared. Pretending I hadn't just spent the last fifteen minutes in a spiral as we made our way to our next location about the last time we had technically been alone together. That had ended with me wanting to disappear into a lint trap and him reminding me that I was just his "little sister's kid best friend."

Nothing was ever going to happen.

The bar was cozy and dimly lit with old-fashioned bulbs strung along the ceiling and a wall of scratched vinyl records behind the bar between televisions blaring the live sports games. The background music was a low, steady hum.

"So," he said, tugging off his jacket again, "how am I doing so far as a fake date?"

I gave him a look. "You get points for showing up. That's already a better track record than most guys these days."

He grinned. "So, I'm winning?"

"It's not a competition."

"Feels like one."

He leaned back on his stool, stretching slightly. His shirt pulled just tight enough to remind me that he had, at some point, become someone with shoulders. Broad ones. Not that I was noticing. Or caring.

"Well then, you're winning. Your competition so far has been your sister."

"I'll take it."

I reached for my water glass before noting my fingers again.

Chuckling at my predicament, Josh handed me a napkin. He looked perfectly at ease, like this wasn't weird. Like none of it was weird.

"Thanks." I took the napkin from him, trying in a some-what-decent effort to wipe the sauce from my fingertips, but really, I think I was just making it worse. "Honestly, I don't think I can count this as a practice date anymore."

Josh smiled at me around another bite of his own dozen wings that he was almost finished with already. "Why not? I'm sure having a good time."

"I would never order wings on a first date."

He looked me over. "Yeah, maybe it's not the best look."

"Hey," I chastised, suddenly feeling a bit self-conscious.

He shook his head as another cheer went up around the bar, and we turned our heads back toward the television screen hanging up behind the rows of liquor bottles and sloping garland someone had attached to either side with hand-tied red velvet bows.

"This is a fun place," I said.

"Not too shabby. Another teacher at school brought me here after I survived my first week a while back. Food is good for bar food and the drinks don't make you hate life."

"A positive," I agreed.

"I thought so too."

As the game on the TV cut to a commercial break, a soft buzz of conversation rose around the bar. It was background noise really—because Josh turned his full attention to me. No distractions. No half watching the screen.

His eyes did a slow sweep over me, like he was trying to figure out something. Like I was unfamiliar and familiar, all at once.

"I never got to ask you," he said finally.

"Ask me what?"

"What you've been up to the past few years." His tone was casual, but there was something behind it. Something heavier. "It's been a while. How have you been, Brielle?"

He said my name softly, like it belonged to him. Just like he used to. And just like then, it knocked the air from my lungs.

I gave him a wary smile. "Besides the obvious?"

He tilted his head, amused. "Avoiding me."

I let out a small scoff. "I haven't been avoiding you."

Josh raised his eyebrows.

"If I was avoiding you, then you were definitely avoiding me," I shot back.

He paused. Then nodded once. "Fair."

I could've pushed. I could've asked why.

Instead, I sighed. "I haven't been doing all that much."

His expression told me he didn't buy that. Not for a second.

"Well, besides the obvious," I conceded.

"I think I've decided I want to hear about the obvious," he said. "Changed my mind."

I rolled my eyes but gave in. "All right. I finished my bachelor's in English—which probably wasn't the best financial decision, but, hey, I did it."

He nodded like he'd heard that part before.

"Then I got into a writing program for my master's. Possibly an even worse decision. I guess I've always been that girl who bets everything on one thing and hopes it works out."

"Why do you say that?"

My finger grazed the rim of my glass. "Because writing was always my thing. I thought doing it in an academic setting would make me better at it—or make it real, I guess. Sometimes, I wonder if it just made me more afraid."

He didn't interrupt. Just listened.

"I had a few pieces published. Little things. Random think pieces and a short essay that did okay. I interned at a small magazine upstate, got my degree, and somehow managed to graduate right alongside Gina, even though we were miles apart. And now ..."

"Now?" he asked gently.

"Now I'm on the never-ending job hunt."

Josh gave a low, thoughtful nod. "You never came back home for Christmas."

"Busy, I guess." I kept my voice even, though my chest tightened. It was true. I had been busy—picking up other people's shifts, taking campus jobs no one wanted. But it wasn't the full truth. The real reason I hadn't come home? I hadn't wanted to walk into the Hutton house again, knowing what had happened the last time I did.

He let the silence hang for a beat. "And now?"

"What do you mean?"

"Are you still busy?" he asked. "Or are you going to come back home?"

I blinked, thrown by the way he had said *home*. Like it was still mine. Like he thought I might still belong there. "I have a new home here."

"You know what I mean."

"I don't know yet," I said. "I guess it depends. If someone hires me soon ..."

"No one's going to start anyone before the new year," he said matter-of-factly.

"Thanks for the vote of confidence."

"I'm serious," he said. "Even if you do get hired, they'll probably start you in January. No one smart kicks off a new employee during the holidays."

I nodded slowly, chewing on that thought. For a few hours, I'd actually managed to forget the weight of my current limbo. Now it was back, settling heavy in my stomach.

"Are you okay?" he asked.

"I have no idea what I'm doing. I mean, is it stupid that I thought after following all the rules, like school and degrees, that gaining experience would be easier? That life would just magically click together once I passed Go and went to work?"

Josh leaned forward, elbows on the table. "No. Definitely not."

I looked at him. "You sure?"

"No one knows what they're doing," he said, serious now. "Everyone's just pretending they've figured it out. The trick is to try to enjoy the pretending."

I stared at him a moment, unsure what to say. I wasn't used to this version of Josh. Thoughtful. Gentle. Still a little infuriating, but now in a way that made my pulse skip.

"Enjoy the pretending."

Easy for him to say. But for some reason, hearing it from him made it feel less like a failure and more like just another stage.

And maybe this—us, here, in this weird fake-date limbo—was just pretending too.

But it didn't feel that way anymore. Or maybe it never would to be. My brain was still probably stuck so many years ago.

"Are you a fortune cookie now?" I countered.

He shrugged with a small laugh.

"And enjoy what pretending? Being a step from an empty bank account and having to explain to your sister that I can't afford a five-dollar pizza night? Not knowing where I am going to end up or if I'm going to be writing articles about anti-aging creams and step-by-steps on how to live a dairy-free, gluten-free lifestyle for the rest of my life? Did you know there are different chocolate sandwich cookies for every kind of dietary restriction these days?"

"Enjoy everything, I guess. Even the not knowing."

I mean, sure, that was easy to say. Too easy. And I was happy I was here. I'd made it to this point in my life, and I was living in a nice apartment with Gina, who I'd still somehow managed to keep as one of my best friends. She was my family, and now we were still together, and it was all I could've ever really asked for.

I was thankful for it.

Grateful.

But was I really enjoying myself as I suffered through employment applications and not doing what a much younger me would've been proud of herself for?

"I mean, you like to write. That's amazing," said Josh. "That's *enjoying*. I've always admired you for that, honestly."

"You have?"

"It's kind of what made me do whatever I wanted to finally two years ago. Among everything else going on."

He admired me?

"You always had a notebook too. Constantly writing in it."

I peered back at him again. "A notebook?"

"Yeah," he said. "Didn't you always check to make sure your bag would be able to hold it?"

I had done that. Or I used to. Now I had my phone I just kept notes on, though I remembered my notebooks. I loved my notebooks even if I thought I might've torn a few of them up during college when I couldn't look at what was inside of them anymore.

I didn't realize that I'd stopped completely until now. I just stopped writing in them. Stopped writing the same stuff anyway, which was probably the entire reason. Because I'd grown as a writer and also because I didn't want to relive the moments I had gotten through. It felt freeing at the time.

Now, I wonder what I would've thought if I looked back at those entries of fairy tales, mixed in with my life I documented each day.

"You always used to have one on you at all times," he said with a chuckle. "I swore, wherever you were, I always knew that I could count on someone having a pen too."

"I forgot I did that."

"Really?"

I nodded. "More or less."

"I can't believe you still don't use a notebook to write. With all your ideas to write, I'm sure it gets crowded up there." He pointed toward my head, nearly poking a saucy finger in the middle of it. "Didn't you say that once before? That you had lots of stories and characters in your head, and sometimes, they felt like they were talking all at once?"

I had. When I wrote stories like that anyway. "I guess I did."

"Don't you still write?"

"Of course I do. I thought you knew that I was trying to find a job to write. That's the city dream after all," I sighed with a bit of hesitancy. The longer I spent trying, the less sure I should continue to.

Writing was solitary, no matter how many people said they were cheering you on in the background after all. In the end, all you had were results. And I didn't have many of those to prove to myself that this was what I was supposed to do, even though writing wasn't what I was supposed to do after spending hours on my computer and years racking up debt and student loans through school ...

What was?

"Hey." Josh ducked his head down to catch my eyes. The longer I thought, the further they drifted down, toward my shoes. "Are you all right? Sorry if I brought something up."

"No. It's fine. It's all good," I assured him. "Sorry. I was just thinking."

Overthinking.

"Like I said, writing hasn't been exactly a dream since I graduated. The first or second time now. The world isn't exactly built for artists who don't know someone who knows someone. Isn't that a phrase?"

He hummed, looking back down at my hands still over my plate of wings. "We definitely need more napkins."

Pulling my brain out of my internal spiral, I glanced down at my sauce-covered fingers. "Yeah."

He reached across the bar counter to commandeer a few.

"Thanks again."

"Means you're eating them right."

"Does it? Or does it just mean that I'm a messy eater?"

He shrugged. "I don't know. Means you're enjoying it."

"Enjoying it again?"

He smiled. "When I travel and try to eat new things, I always have the tendency to make a mess of myself though. Just happens. I have no idea how to stop it, and I've given up on trying."

"People must think you have eating issues."

"Especially when it comes to dessert. I got icing and sweet creams all over myself in France—the ratios were all over the place—but I still couldn't stop myself from trying a new pastry. Or in Asia. Did you know that in some places, it's considered bad form not to slurp when you're eating something good?"

"Really?"

"Maybe. Could just be a lie to weed the Americans out." He pursed his lips, as if considering this new thought before offering another laugh.

I was unsure if I'd ever heard Josh laugh this much in his entire life. At least not while I was around. It was a good look for him. The sun-kissed freckles he must've developed against his tanned skin. The way his voice dipped when he chuckled. The laugh lines around his mouth he didn't try to hide.

"Either way, the ramen went down great," he said.

I laughed. "That good?"

"Best ever. Be disappointed if it wasn't."

"It was worth it though?"

"The noodles?"

"The travel," I said. "The up and leaving your good job and running away."

"I wouldn't say it was running away."

"What would you call it then?"

"Changing." Josh said the word as if it was simple. "For the better. So, yeah, eating noodles across the world and stuffing my face full of various desserts definitely made me a better person. A better life liver."

"Life liver?" I questioned.

"It's a word."

"I don't doubt you," I said. "Wasn't it scary though? Taking such a risk?"

"I figure that's half the fun, Bri. You should know that. You took the biggest risk of us all straight out of school and look at you now."

"Look at me now? Broke in the city, living with my best friend and her brother."

"Living in the city."

Be grateful.

Be happy.

"And eating pretty decent wings with me," he added.

That was, oddly enough, more than good right now. It was one of the best feelings I'd had in a while since I'd arrived. Not so ... alone.

Not responding, I took the moment to eat a piece of neglected celery off to the side.

It felt nice to talk with Josh. More than nice. Yet still, I couldn't help but think of our last conversation we'd had years ago. That, too, was hanging over me with a new wave of awkwardness.

"Josh?" I debated asking him if he remembered. If ... he ... I didn't know what, but I just wanted to ...

"Hey!"

A tall figure cut between us before I even had time to register what was happening. One broad arm clapped around Josh's shoulders with the force of a reunion long overdue.

"Good to see you, man! How've you been?"

Josh blinked, then broke into a grin. "Hunter. Wow. Hey, man. It's been a minute."

"I was uptown for a late meeting," Hunter explained, already making himself at home as he leaned slightly over the table. "Figured I'd catch the end of the game here. Not like I missed much though."

Josh shook his head, chuckling. "Yeah, this one's been a bit of a snooze."

Then Hunter's eyes landed on me. His suit, dark and sleek, screamed finance—or something adjacent to it. I could practically see the old photos Gina used to show me of Josh during his corporate days. The same clean lines. The same city-boy edge.

Hunter nudged Josh, smirking. "And who's this?"

Josh didn't look at me right away. "This is Brielle. She's friends with my sister."

Hunter's grin grew wide. "Ohhhh, look at you. Keeping it in the family, huh? I told you, you weren't going to be the one who ended up alone out of the lot of us."

I raised my brows. Was there a bet?

Josh let out a small, tight laugh. "No, it's not—we're not together."

The way he said it though, clipped and quick, sent a weird jolt through me. Like he was trying to clean something up or shoo me away like I was someone who jumped up onstage drunk to sing karaoke and he assured the people at the bar, *I don't know her.*

"We pretty much grew up together. She's practically another sister."

Another sister.

There it was.

I forced a small smile, nodding politely at Hunter.

Hunter, blissfully unaware of the chaos rolling through my head, laughed. "Well, whatever it is, good for you, man. I'm just glad to see you out in the world again."

I wasn't sure what that meant. And I didn't ask.

Because all I could hear, echoing louder than the game coming back on the TVs overhead, was that word again.

Sister.

Maybe this whole fake-date thing wasn't such a good idea after all. I suddenly was having a whole new irritating wave toward Gina again.

Josh waved between himself and Hunter. "We used to work together."

"I figured." I cleared my throat and almost extended my hand before remembering the wings. "Sorry. Nice to meet you. Yeah, I definitely annoyed this guy enough, growing up."

"That's fun. You guys are just out enjoying the game then at least? Your team is getting cooked."

"My sister bailed on her."

"What a great guy," his friend said, pulling him into what looked like a headlock. "You know what a good guy my friend is?"

I nodded, glancing toward Josh again, who was staring at me. It looked like he hadn't stopped looking at me with that soft, understanding smile on his face that might've been pity after our conversation. Again. Wow.

"Oh," I said, "I know."

six

"THANK YOU," I said. "For hanging out or whatever."

Josh offered a swift nod of his head as we came upon my apartment door. Our apartment. "Hey, I take great honor in being your first date, Brielle."

I paused. "Practice date."

"Basically the most important."

"Sure," I offered a laugh and a shrug. "Sorry it took up your whole evening."

"I had a great time. What are you talking about?"

Right, I was sure he had.

"I mean, I'm glad I could help." Josh let out a low whistle. "Gina's trying to get you cuffed before Christmas. Ruthless."

"When you put it that way ..."

"It was also good to talk with you again, Brielle."

I opened my mouth and paused. Tried again.

"Well, I guess I'll"—I pointed toward my room—"get out of your room now."

He shrugged, leaning back on the couch. "You could watch TV if you want. I feel bad that I pushed you guys out of your new space. I've been meaning to tell you that this space is as much yours as it is mine, but with you avoiding me and all, I kind of left it up to you."

Again, I didn't correct him that I hadn't been. But now, as I stood there, looking at him—

"Unless you are still avoiding me."

So, that was the game we were playing.

He had laid down the challenge, casual and cool from his corner of the couch, like he hadn't just dared me to cross some invisible line neither of us had talked about yet.

I glanced toward my bedroom door. I could have retreated, shut it behind me, and spared myself the confusion that came with this new version of Josh—so familiar and yet so different.

Instead, I let out a quiet huff and peeled off my jacket, hanging it on the hook by the door. One layer down. One excuse less.

Slowly, I padded across the room. He'd done a decent job today, cleaning up the chaos that usually made the couch look like a lumpy bed. But as I sat down, sinking into the cushion beside him, that was all I could see.

I was sitting on his bed.

With him.

"Feel good to be sitting in your own living room again?" he asked, voice low and teasing.

"Never really had one before," I admitted.

"What? Not even in college?"

I shook my head. "Nope. I mostly relied on dorms and what my financial aid would cover. A lot of shared common rooms and ancient furniture that smelled like leftover ramen and broken dreams. Not exactly HGTV material."

Josh winced, his smile twisting. "Now I feel even worse for taking up this space. I'll be out of your hair soon though."

"I'm sure," I said lightly, even though I wasn't.

"Don't worry; I'm not leaving the city," he said, misreading the pause. "Just looking for another place."

I opened my mouth to ask where, but he beat me to it.

"Maybe I'll have you come check out the next one. Y'know, since you're the authority on non-homey spaces."

I blinked, caught off guard. The words weren't cruel, but they hit something soft in me anyway.

He noticed immediately. "Sorry. That came out wrong."

"No, it's okay," I said quickly. And maybe it was. Maybe it wasn't. "If you need someone to apartment-hunt with, you ..." I trailed off, pulling my legs up onto the couch, wrapping my arms around my knees until I was a small ball of uncertainty. "I wouldn't mind being that person."

Josh turned slightly, eyes meeting mine. A beat passed— quiet, but heavy with something unspoken.

Then, softly, "Sure."

"Thanks."

Shifting on the couch my feet brushed up against his leg. He jumped at the touch.

"Sorry."

"Holy shit. Are those your toes?"

"Sorry," I said, trying to adjust again so that they were tucked better under me. "I know they're cold."

"They are like ice cubes. Do you have socks on?"

"I run cold."

He lifted the blanket that he had yanked down from behind his head. Before I could argue, he was already unraveling it, laying it across his lap as well as my own. "Get under here."

Slowly, I did.

"Thanks."

He didn't mention it, lifting the remote to the screen and letting it flare to life. "I do have a show I've been meaning to watch if you want—"

The door to the apartment creaked open.

"I'm sorry I forced you to sit through your practice date with my brother. I know, worst-friend status!" Gina called out as she entered, shrugging off her coat like the wind had offended her personally.

She glanced between the two of us. "You okay?"

"Just—"

"Recapping our evening," Josh jumped in smoothly. "So, your dear friend, who you so generously subjected to my company tonight, can go into her blind dates with confidence."

Gina narrowed her eyes at him. She didn't look convinced.

I stood from the couch. The edge of the blanket I'd tucked around my feet—and the quiet touch of Josh's hand—slipped away.

Did I imagine the way his fingers had lingered for just a second longer, like they didn't want to let go?

"I'm about to head to bed," I said, ignoring the way my chest suddenly ached with the loss of that small warmth. I didn't look back as I stepped toward my room.

Gina followed. "So? How'd it go? How was the restaurant I'd picked out?"

"We ended up going to the bar for wings."

"Ugh. Do you have no class, Josh? Seriously?" she called out the door.

Josh didn't respond.

She turned back to me, expecting backup.

"The wings were good," I admitted. "Sweet chili."

"You're too nice," she scoffed. Then she softened. "But I'm glad you guys didn't kill each other. I mean, it's good that you two are finally on better terms. Especially since we're all living together now—and spending Christmas at home."

"I still don't know if I'm coming home, Gina. I've got a lot to do here."

"Lies," she declared. "I'm not leaving you here alone. I let you make excuses for years, but unless one of your blind dates ends in a spontaneous elopement to Fiji, you're coming. I already told my mom you were."

I stared at her. "How was work?"

Her face lit up instantly, eyes bright and excited. "You won't believe the installation we're getting last minute this month. You should take one of your dates there."

First, I thought, *I have to actually go on one of them.*

Though the idea didn't hit quite the same anymore. My heart was still gently pounding from earlier, like it hadn't caught up with the rest of me. I told myself it was just the adrenaline from going out, talking, socializing again.

But I knew what it was.

Josh.

I shook it off. "Guess we'll see. You'll have to send me the info."

"You'll hear about it," she promised, practically bouncing. "I'm just so excited for you. This is your moment. But I still think you should start a new blog series or something. Like, document everything—job-hunting, dates, all of it. It's content gold."

I groaned. "You want me to write about my dating woes?"

"Who says they'll be woes? Could be ups and downs. It's relatable! You liked Josh and his pub wings, didn't you? It only gets better from there, right?"

She wasn't totally wrong. I *had* liked tonight. More than I should've.

"Everyone likes a dating adventure," she went on. "It's basically what *Sex and the City* was built on. You're a real writer. Own it."

"I see where you're going with this."

"Maybe a magazine picks it up. Or it rounds out your portfolio, like you've been talking about."

"I just don't know if I want to put my whole life out there."

"Think of them as stories," she said, already scheming. "Or a newsletter. Newsletters are hot these days."

"I don't write stories anymore."

"Doesn't mean you can't. Or won't again. I remember when you used to write all the time."

"Josh said that too," I murmured.

Her eyebrows shot up. "See? Even he remembers. That should mean something."

"I'll think about it."

She pursed her lips, like she knew she'd won at least part of the argument. "This is going to be the best month we've ever had in the city. I can feel it. Isn't there a saying or something?"

"Like what?"

"Holidays in the city. It's where dreams come true."

"I think that's Disney, Gina."

She just grinned the same mischievous grin she and her brother shared. "Whatever. Don't back down now. It's going to be great."

12 THE DATES TILL CHRISTMAS

BY BRIELLE THOMPSON

INTRODUCTION

There are usually only two reasons people agree to go on blind dates: because they trust their friends who want to set them up, and, well, because they're desperate.

To be honest, I wasn't sure which category I fell into until after Date One (more to come on that).

This had all started when my best friend—who also happens to be my roommate and an unapologetic romantic masochist—decided that my love life needed a glow-up. Apparently, being single in your twenties while job-hunting and eating dry toast over your laptop doesn't scream thriving.

Who knew?

So, she and her friends made a list for me. Twelve names. Twelve men. Who they insist have "potential." Allegedly, mind you. After today, well, I'm skeptical.

I agreed under one condition. No lengthy bios of potential suitors, no filters, no pre-date Instagram stalking that would make me second guess all of this in one fell swoop. Just a time, a place, and a first name. A proper experiment.

Ready?

I'm not sure if I am.

seven

WAS it bad that I couldn't stop thinking about the other night with Josh?

Probably.

It was stupid. How, after all of two or three hours together, did I somehow become just as ridiculous as the girl I had been in high school ... and the first two years of college? That girl who'd practically curated an entire mental museum of moments about her best friend's older brother.

After that Christmas, I'd sworn I was done with him.

I *was*. Sort of.

I didn't carry around embarrassment or heartbreak—not really. Instead, I funneled all those years of feelings into something sharper, easier to hold on to. Irritation. Annoyance. A thin layer of cold indifference that kept me safe.

But now?

Josh was here. Again.

Right in front of me. In my apartment. Sitting on my couch. Asking me about my day like he hadn't wrecked me once without even trying.

Somehow, that bitterness I had cultivated so carefully over

time? It was already starting to melt. Which made no sense. I shouldn't just forgive him. I shouldn't move on like that night had never happened.

But why did it feel like doing so would be the easiest thing in the world?

Maybe because I already had.

We weren't avoiding each other anymore. Not even a little.

When he came home from school and saw me still in my pajamas, half buried in a Word doc and a pile of career rejection emails, he didn't laugh.

He asked me how my day was, like it was normal.

I asked him how his day was too.

And somehow, that became routine.

This week, he'd even cooked for us. Multiple nights. Real food, not just microwaveable garbage or emergency toast, slathered with unsalted stick butter.

He bought the groceries himself and didn't ask us for money to split.

I'd been keeping a mental tally of what I owed him anyway. I promised myself that once I had a job—or an interview, anything—I'd cook something simple in return. Maybe spaghetti. Maybe I'd splurge on that stupid artisan bread I always passed at the front of the grocery store and never bought.

Tonight though? Josh had looked at me. Really looked.

Gina had spent the last two hours doing my hair, fixing my makeup, and demanding that I not wear a single piece of clothing made of elastic. When I stepped out, even Josh stared. But he didn't say anything.

He stared.

I pretended not to notice.

He didn't say a word.

Now, I was standing at a cozy little Italian restaurant in

West Town, trying not to visibly panic as I gave a name I didn't know to a hostess who led me to a table where I didn't know who to look for.

This was the guy Brent had set me up with.

Brent claimed he was "perfect" for me. Apparently, he was looking to settle down. Which was ... weirdly adult. And not necessarily a selling point.

At least it meant he likely wasn't a total creep. Right?

I hoped.

I took a breath. Smoothed down my dress.

Then I saw him. For some reason, I was shocked.

For some reason, I was taken aback. He looked cute.

Really cute.

He had dirty-blond hair that was styled enough that it was clear he'd put some effort into how he looked for our date and wore a blue collared shirt that, on anyone else, I might've thought they had gotten it as a gift. The rest of his outfit looked just as put together as he stood up with a wide, very white smile.

"Hey, you made it!"

"I made it," I responded, trying my own smile that felt a little like I was trying to stretch my face into a strange expression, especially with the new dark lip stain that was slowly drying out my lips.

I'd tried to tell Gina that I was pretty sure I looked like a goth clown.

She had insisted otherwise. "Just let me have my moment, making you up! It's just like old times, isn't it?"

It had been. And I trusted her.

I needed to calm down and take a deep breath.

Dates were just dates. This was just a date. I hadn't been this nervous when Josh plopped himself down across from me in one of Gina's social-media-worthy restaurants. And this place was much cozier.

"It's really good to meet you. I'm Trevor," he introduced himself.

I moved toward the table, hesitating at his open arms. Oh, I was supposed to give him a hug.

God, am I really so rusty at this dating thing?

Gina's intent for Josh to prep me for date number one already was failing me as I gently patted his back and stepped away.

He waved toward the table, half taking out my seat.

Huh, a gentleman?

For some reason, I hadn't expected that.

Maybe this blind-date nonsense that Gina had in mind wasn't such an awful idea after all.

"I'm Brielle."

"Good, or else I just hugged the wrong person."

He laughed, and I tried to give a laugh as well, though it came out a little forced. Luckily, he didn't seem to notice the extra effort.

Count that as a win.

"How are you?" He asked.

"I'm doing pretty good," I said. "How are you?"

"Doing just fine. I was kind of questioning this—I'm not going to lie. I only ever hear about blind-date horror stories."

"You aren't the only one. It's nice to meet you though."

"Likewise. Have you been here before?"'

"Nope. I just moved in, sort of, a few months ago. I'm still recouping some moving costs, along with exploring everywhere."

"It's great here. I really like their pasta dishes. Their cacio e pepe is solid."

"I love pasta anything," I said, glancing down at the menu in front of me. "You have good taste in carbs."

Not to mention, I was starving. I hadn't eaten all day, both from nerves and trying to keep myself working on my computer to distract myself from how I hadn't picked up groceries for the coming week yet.

He winked. "I aim to please my dates."

"You've brought other dates here?" I lifted my eyes away from the menu, though I knew what I was getting based on his recommendation alone, if my stomach would stop buzzing like it was full of bees. Was it normal to be this nervous?

"Oh, yeah. I mean, the food is amazing, and it's not too overwhelming. I guess that's kind of bad on my part, huh?"

I shook my head. "No. If the food is that good, definitely not. And if you have a spot you're comfortable with, I don't blame you."

He chuckled, reaching to rub the back of his neck. "Glad I didn't just strike myself out there within the first ten minutes."

"All good. Definitely not."

Man, was warm in here?

I shrugged my coat from my shoulders.

Trevor gave a low whistle, just loud enough for me to hear. Still, I glanced either way to see if anyone else was looking. My cheeks heated.

"Sorry," he excused himself. "You look beautiful."

I shifted in my seat, trying to get comfortable again. I went with the top Gina had suggested—the sheer black sleeves dipping low over my shoulders. "Thank you."

"You know what you want here?"

"Um ..." I glanced at the menu.

I'd already studied it at home, determined not to embarrass myself. This place was one of those tiny, unassuming restaurants everyone online swore by—especially for their wine pairings.

It felt a little extravagant for a first blind date. But I figured, why not start strong? Besides, I had a good feeling about the last job I'd applied to. For once, the reply didn't feel like a form rejection. They said they'd be in touch for the next steps.

Maybe things were finally turning around.

"She just sat down. She isn't ready yet," Trevor said.

I blinked.

So did the server.

"Oh, sorry," she murmured, taking a step back.

"You can give us a minute," he added, not even looking at her as she backed away. "Thanks."

"Of course," she said, slipping her notepad into her apron and turning toward another table.

I tried to smile after her, a little embarrassed. "It's okay," I told him. "I actually did look at the menu earlier. Or, if you've been here before, I trust your opinion."

He didn't respond to that.

Instead, he snapped his fingers. *Snapped.*

"Hey. When you get a second, we're ready," he called, again without even glancing in her direction.

The server's polite smile didn't meet her eyes. I recognized that look—tight and practiced. Trevor didn't seem to notice. Or care as he rattled off to start with bread and the house salad. "Whatever dressing." Before he looked away from her without a single thank you.

"Do you know her?" I asked.

"What?" He blinked at me like I'd interrupted something. "Who?"

I stared. Was he serious? "The server."

His brow furrowed. "No. Why?"

"It's just … how you talked to her. I thought maybe you were joking after first." Or at least trying to joke. God, I hoped he'd just been awkward.

"Ah, okay." He nodded like he understood now. Like I was the one who'd overreacted. He leaned back in his seat, settling in. "It's fine."

It was?

"I used to work in a restaurant," he asserted. "I know how things work. They want to get in and out. Turn tables around you know. This way all of *this* is efficient." He vaguely gestured around our table.

"You do," I echoed. It wasn't really a question. More of a ... processing noise.

He shrugged. "Yeah. It's fine."

We sat in silence for a moment. It wasn't fine.

But I wasn't sure if it was worth saying that out loud yet. Or if this was just a weird hiccup. First dates were supposed to be a little awkward, right?

Still ...

The way he'd said "efficient" made something in my stomach flip, and not in a good way.

eight

I KICKED OFF MY BOOTS, nearly swearing as I did at the immediate relief. My toes were sore and—was that a blister?

I let out a groan.

So much for my attempt to look nice for my first blind date. If dating was anything like this from here on out, I was going to need a serious investment in insoles.

The apartment was quiet, except for the faint hum of the heater and the buzz of a lamp still on in the living room. I half expected Josh to be camped out on the couch again, watching something with the subtitles on.

But it was empty.

Just as I was about to disappear into my room, a door creaked open.

"Bri?" Gina whispered like I was breaking curfew.

In fact, I was early. More than early. I hadn't made it past that first drink before I made an excuse to get out of here.

"You're home."

I sighed. Busted. "Yeah. No one is here."

She stepped into the hallway, looking toward the living

room, as if she noticed it was just them as well. She was already in mismatched pajamas and a silk scrunchie on her wrist. "So? Tell me everything. Was he cute?"

"He was cute," I admitted, toeing the floorboard near the radiator like it might offer me answers. "Kind of a textbook cute."

"Ooh, like an investment-banker cute or dog-dad cute?"

"Like you'd easily see him in a dental-commercial cute," I settled on. Little tooth sparkles and everything.

"That doesn't sound bad," she began slowly, smart enough to know that this wasn't yet the deal-breaker.

"It wasn't bad," I said. Then paused. "Not exactly."

She narrowed her eyes. "Don't hold back. I know you are waiting to say something, and I can tell it is going to be a doozy. What happened?"

I shrugged off my coat and let it fall onto the chair, collapsing into the corner of the couch. "I think he was rude."

"To you?"

"No. To the server."

Her face twisted like I'd handed her a sour candy. "Ugh."

"I know."

"What'd he do?"

"He basically waved her off when I was about to order. Told her I wasn't ready. Then he snapped his fingers at her later. And when I called it out, he said it was fine because he used to work in a restaurant, so he knows how it is."

"Snapped?" Gina echoed. "Like dog-training snapped?"

"Yep."

"Oh, hell no."

"That's what I thought. But then I kept second-guessing myself because he didn't do it to me and maybe I was being too sensitive?"

"No. No, no, no." She waved a finger. "Brielle. Rule number

one. You can tell who someone is by how they treat people they don't need to impress. And if I was that server? Yeesh. He would've gotten a piece of my mind because we both know that he wouldn't have tipped anyway."

I nodded, but it didn't feel like it should have mattered this much. It had been one date. A few hours. I shouldn't have felt this heavy after.

Still, I felt ... tired. Like I'd wasted something intangible I couldn't quite name.

"He kept acting like he was doing me a favor just by being there. But also like I should be impressed by him. Like I was the one who needed to catch up. I don't know. It was weird."

Gina sat next to me and leaned her head on my shoulder. "That sucks. But, hey, you wore heels. That's a big deal. You left the apartment. That's all a win."

I snorted. "It's a low bar."

"Dating is a low bar. Welcome back to the trenches, babe." She bumped her shoulder against mine. "Seriously though, you did it. You got through the first one. And the next guy might be a total gem. Or, you know, not a finger-snapper."

"Small victories," I murmured.

"And, hey, if nothing else"—she looked up at me with that wicked grin she shared with her brother—"this is going to make great newsletter material."

I groaned, but even as I rolled my eyes, I felt it. The tiny seed of relief from telling someone.

And somewhere deep beneath the awkward tension and the sore feet was that other feeling again.

The one I kept pretending not to notice whenever I walked past Josh's room.

The one that bloomed when he asked me how my day was.

That was a problem for later.

nine

THE SECOND THE bathroom door clicked shut behind me, I turned on the water and stripped off the outfit Gina had painstakingly chosen for my first date. The curls she had given me were already limp from the cold wind outside and smelled like a little bit of garlic from the restaurant.

Soap couldn't scrub that out of my memory, but I gave it my best shot.

By the time I emerged from the shower, wrapped in my pajamas and robe, hair damp and hanging limp, I felt marginally more like a person again.

Gina's bedroom door was cracked open and dark. She must've gone to bed already. Her work had required early morning wake-up calls this past week.

I padded quietly into the living room, expecting it to be quiet.

It wasn't.

Josh was there stretched out on his sofa bed, remote lifted to pause the screen in one of his old hoodies. The TV volume low and a half-empty glass of water on the coffee table in front of him.

He looked up when he heard me. "Hey."

I blinked, caught slightly off guard. "Hi. I thought you were out for the night."

The apartment was cast in a low glow from the television and light above the stove.

"Oh, sorry. I didn't mean to interrupt your decompressing time."

He shook his head. "Decompressing time?"

I shrugged.

"How was your date?"

"Oh, that."

Josh cocked his head. "I take it, it didn't go well?"

"It was ... short."

His eyes remained snagged on me, not moving to return his full attention to his television show, which ... I had been wanting to see actually. A new sort of drama-thriller combination everyone had been talking about online.

I pointed at the screen as I made my way toward his couch bed. I dropped into the old armchair next to it. Gina and I found the plush chair at the thrift store not too long after we moved in. The floral pattern was a little tacky, but it was one of the first things we got together to decorate. Plus, I'll never forget the two of us complaining and laughing the entire climb up the stairs to the apartment.

Josh glanced at the TV, but didn't really seem to be watching it anymore. "You okay?"

I looked at him. "I will be," I said honestly. "I think I just expected to feel something different tonight. I thought maybe the first date would make me excited. You know, give me that stupid butterflies feeling that people talk about."

"And it didn't?" he said.

"Not even close."

"Sorry."

I shook my head. "Can I watch with you?"

Josh was still looking at me, scanning me in my layers of loungewear.

One episode, and then I'd call it a night.

"You got it. Want me to catch you up on what's happening? Or we can just restart it. I'm not that far in."

"Really?"

"Yeah."

I sighed with a nod, sinking lower into the chair. "That would be amazing."

THE
DATES TILL CHRISTMAS

BY BRIELLE THOMPSON

DATE ONE

Location: Cozy Italian spot with dim lighting and an overachieving wine list.
First Impression: Cute. Great jawline. Button-down shirt that looked expensive, but somehow still had wine spilled on the cuff. (Probably from a past date he'd brought to the same place.)

Promising start. But then ... You know that weird instinct you get when a customer speaks to a server like they're imagining what life would be like if they suddenly became a billionaire who can't decipher a normal person's social cues?

They guy didn't yell. But the snapping? Literally. He snapped his fingers! The condescending tone? The "I've worked in a restaurant, so I know" energy and actual excuse?

I should've ordered my Alfredo to go.

Because I did ... go. I didn't even make it to the crusty bread portion which left me more disappointed than the actual date, come to think of it.

I got home, took a shower and ended up lounging on the couch watching a new with my best friend's brother who has been couch-surfing with us for the past month.

Blind Date Status: Swooned at the idea of getting dressed up. Survived. Developing a theory that the cuter the guy, the worse his restaurant etiquette.

At the end of the week, I'll be meeting someone who "loves animals" and "has golden-retriever energy." Here's hoping he doesn't treat waitstaff like they are his personal servants in a period drama.

ten

SOMEONE WHISPERED TO ME, but I couldn't hear what they were saying. I did, however, feel the hands that were coming up behind my back and my knees, jostling me awake.

I hummed a sound as my eyes opened, realizing that I was being lifted. Though that made no sense.

Where was I?

A familiar chuckle cut into my thoughts as I gathered my bearings.

"Now you wake up? I don't remember you being a heavy sleeper, Bri. I got ya."

"Sorry. I fell asleep. Again." It was becoming a habit lately after I came in late at night. Josh would see me, ask how my date went to which I gave him few details, and then we'd watch another episode or two or three of our show.

"Eh, we'll just have to watch the last episode again later. I fell asleep too."

He walked me the few steps to my room before he paused in the threshold. I looked up at him before he seemed to clear his throat, stepping past the threshold and into my room. My bed was still unmade from this morning. The few possessions I had were cramped in the small space, yet it was all mine in a way that I hadn't had my own room since I moved out and went to college.

Slowly, leaning over, Josh set me down on my bed, swinging the yellow gingham comforter back. With a jerk of his chin, I followed the direction to put my feet inside. Though Josh wasn't quite done yet as he diligently tucked me in, starting at my legs. Leaning over me, he braced his hands on the edge of my bed, causing the mattress to dip toward him, and I didn't move.

My head rolled toward him on my pillow, and my hair got caught under my shoulder, but I didn't adjust. I was too fixated on the way the streetlight outside my window cast a glow across Josh's face, where his eyes were staring directly back at me.

In the quiet, with his face so close to mine I could hear his breathing, even above the gentle rumble of cars and distant sirens blaring outside in the city's version of white noise.

I swallowed, and that seemed to be enough for the two of us to snap out of whatever trance between sleep and awake we had been in this entire time. Eyes widening before he cleared his throat, Josh stood up, fixing a corner of my blanket, as if that had been his intention a few seconds ago, which had felt like an eternity.

Or was it really just me feeling that wasn't all that was happening here between us?

Again?

I shut my eyes as I gathered my composure. Taking a breath, I blinked my eyes back open. "Thanks."

Josh—my best friend's brother, who I felt like I was millimeters away from kissing in my bedroom in the apartment we shared—smiled, looking around the room one more time before he turned around and walked right back out the door to the living room.

"Night."

THE 12 DATES TILL CHRISTMAS

BY BRIELLE THOMPSON

DATE FOUR

Location: Rooftop bar with fake snow machines and overpriced cocktails.

First Impression: This date was suggested by my friend's coworker, who said he was "sweet, funny, and emotionally available." I should've known that was code for weird but in an endearing way. Or just ... weird.

I went in a little unsure, but Date Four was sweet. Like, aggressively sweet. He asked me questions, laughed at my jokes (even the bad ones), and told me that he once cried rewatching his favorite children's movie. The whole about him should've worked.

However, halfway through the night, I noticed something strange.

His socks.

Okay, don't judge me when I say this. His socks were alarming. One was pink with detailed illustrations of shrimp cocktail, and the other had tiny photos of Pedro Pascal. Neither matched his outfit.

When I asked about them, he looked me dead in the eye and said, and I quote, "Sometimes, my feet like to go on different adventures. Fun, right?"

What does that mean, Date Four?

Blind Date Status: Emotionally available. Possibly writing a manifesto via a quirky sock Etsy shop. I think it would be good for him. Would I see Date Four again? Probably not. But I do hope his feet found their way home.

And, hey, at least he would've been easy to buy a gift for.

eleven

"ARE you sure this is the place you wanted to go?" I yelled over the loud music playing through the speakers.

When I had thought of the "holiday bar," as Jackson had described it over the phone—which made me feel like maybe this guy might not be another obnoxious dud (positive thinking going out into the world and all that)—this place on the corner of a street I was unsure I'd ever traveled to before in daylight wasn't it.

Though the place had old garland and slightly withered red ribbons—which were fading to something closer to pink—decorating the bar, the music was anything but the holiday-themed drinks date number two, Jackson, had promised. In fact, the only way to describe this bar in particular was a dive.

I wasn't picky or anything, but for some reason, I was thinking back to my first date—no, *practice* date with Josh and the Jingle Bell Martini on the menu. The more I thought about it, the more it didn't actually sound that bad.

In fact, I was pretty sure I would love one right now.

"Yeah, this place is great!" Jackson yelled back, unperturbed that he had to. "Plus, like I said, the drinks are dirt cheap!"

"I thought you said that it was a holiday place?"

"I'm sure they have something!" He pushed us through the thick crowd of people stuffed inside the building until we reached the front, where bartenders were pouring over lines of tequila shots with lime.

At a house party, I wouldn't think twice about it, and yet I was still looking for any sign of Christmas cheer here other than Jackson's red striped flannel he wore open with a black tee shirt peeking out from underneath.

All I managed to see was Christmas depression, which, honestly, was starting to match my mood as of late.

Over the past two weeks, I had gone on five dates. Five. After the first douche canoe, I'd made sure that I wasn't going to let myself get stuck in a possible three-course meal.

My last date (or was it two dates ago? I was already getting them mixed up.) had been polite, but talked about his mom. A lot. For our date, we painted mugs at a paint-and-create studio. It was his idea, which I loved, and I was still excited to pick up my final creation whenever they called. But by the end, I had known his mom's favorite color, holiday, astrological sign, and health history—where he was still concerned about how she always managed to get the flu each year, no matter what she did, even with all the herbal, holistic stuff she tried, except for quarantining herself away from humanity.

Another date had taken a scheduled phone call halfway through the date and then seemed shocked when I ate half the soft pretzel he'd ordered for us. After nearly a half hour of waiting for him to return to the table, I wanted to sneak out the door and leave, but he was blocking the exit as he chortled with whoever he was talking with, who clearly had more interesting things to discuss than I did by that point.

Another date had been shocked that I was freelancing at the moment though he'd seemed ok with it.

"*So, you're unemployed,*" he corrected.

"*Not completely.*" Though ... *kinda.*

I'd had a two-day break before getting another one-off job of writing copy for a website selling bespoke lingerie, which was actually pretty fun after the owner said to give it a sweet and spicy tone.

Oddly enough, after posting on my newsletter about date number two, I had been accumulating more followers on my platform than I could've ever expected. Lots of people related to the bad or simply sub-optimal dates and were all too happy to add their own jokes. A few people started to question just how real my experiences in the newsletter were, but were hooked nonetheless.

I had readers!

I might not have had a job still, and I felt like I was relying on Josh staying with us to split the rent three ways now more than ever, but I had actual people reading my writing, and for some reason, my heart hammered with excitement every time I got a notification for another one.

I hadn't given up on the job search either amongst all of this. On the contrary, I'd also sent over twenty job applications. I heard back from one, who informed me that the pay was barely enough to cover my MetroCard for the month, let alone rent and groceries, and there were also no benefits, but they were looking for someone with a master's degree and a flexible schedule, so I'd be a great fit!

I was beginning to feel that the only place I was a great fit was akin to a trash shoot.

Or a dive bar.

"What do you want?"

Honestly, I was about to say I'd like to leave.

I took a deep breath. I was going to give this a chance. It would be wrong not to. So what if all my other dates hadn't exactly gone to plan and only proved that all the good guys in the world were truly taken—a very sad fact for someone only in their mid-twenties?

I was not going to ruin something—if there even was something here—just because Jackson was someone who enjoyed an off-the-beaten-path location. The city was full of unique bars.

Maybe this was one of them, and I just didn't know it yet.

Positive thinking.

"What was that?" I asked, blinking as I refocused on Jackson, taking in how he had a rather delightful spattering of freckles up the sides of his face and deep, hooded brown eyes.

He gave me a hesitant, crooked smile and looked at me up and down again, as if he was deciding what was wrong with me that I had to ask again. "What do you want to drink?"

I heard him that time. "I'll just have a vodka cranberry."

He gave me an A-okay sign with his fingers.

Great.

He shouted over the noise at the bartender before both of our glasses—his a beer—were slid over. "Here you go."

"Thanks."

"Oh, wait."

He reached for it back, and unsure of what else to do, I let him take it, watching the dull glimmer of the glass as it was exchanged between us. Then he took a sip out of my drink.

Right through the thin straw.

I was certain that I couldn't help the way my eyes widened.

"Tastes good. Just wanted you to know that it was safe and everything."

He had taken a sip of my drink to ... show me that he hadn't drugged me?

I took the slightly dingy-looking glass back and took a big gulp of it, trying not to think of any backwash possibilities.

He was right at the very least. It was good. Strong.

I had a feeling that I was going to need it if I was going to make it through tonight, though I quickly shot a text to Gina.

> I may need an SOS.

No!

> Yes.

Why???

> Just a feeling.

And a whole lot of other reasons.

A few dots popped up for a new response, but I quickly slid my phone back into my pocket and out of view.

"Sorry about that—"

I stopped myself as I looked up and noticed that my date had already moved on to the other end of the bar. He was talking to another woman, who gave him a tight hug.

What in the world was going on here?

"Hey, Brenna," Jackson called, seeing me, waving me closer.

"It's Brielle," I corrected him.

"What?"

What did he have me saved in his phone as?

I raised my voice, hoping that maybe I hadn't heard him right. "My name is Brielle!"

"That's what I said. This is Cassie."

I blinked at the girl in front of me with long, wavy hair. "Hi."

She looked me up and down with confusion on her face that I was pretty sure mirrored my own. "Um, hi."

Then Jackson didn't say anything else. But he did talk to her. "So, where were we again?"

"You just asked me if I have been in the city for long. I said that I have been here for the past three years," she said.

"And you?" He turned to me for my answer.

"I just moved here in August," I answered hesitantly.

What was going on here? This wasn't an interview, but Jackson was sure treating it as one, looking between the two of us. I wouldn't call myself the most date-savvy, but after my last two weeks of dates, but—

"Wait a second."

He raised his eyebrows.

"Are you on a date with her?"

twelve

AS SOON AS the realization hit me, it sank in like a slap to the face.

"You're on a date with both of us? At the same time? Here?" My voice was colder than the wind outside.

Of all places. Here?

Jackson nodded like I'd just asked him if he wanted fries with his meal. "Yeah."

Cassie's eyes went wide, her mouth half open, as if the words were caught somewhere in her throat. "What?"

"I don't get the big deal," Jackson said with a casual shrug, glancing between us like we were the weird ones.

Around us, conversations at nearby tables began to dip. People were starting to catch on. I could feel their stares behind me, the pause in their laughter.

"We're all just trying to find someone, right? It's not like I knew either of you before tonight. This way's just more efficient."

Efficient.

He said it like it was a spreadsheet and not two actual human beings sitting across from him with real expectations and at least a little bit of hope. His tone was matter-of-fact, even bored.

A lot like date number one.

They really were not all that original.

Cassie's face twisted in disbelief. "You do realize that's not how dates work, right?"

Jackson rolled his eyes like we were being dramatic. "Whatever. I don't need someone more uptight than I already am."

Uptight. I smiled—tight, sharp, teeth baring.

"Right," I said, lifting my nearly empty vodka cran and draining it in one long gulp. I set it down with a satisfying clink. "Thanks for the drink."

Then I turned and walked away without looking back.

Behind me, I could hear Cassie mutter under her breath, "Such an asshole," before she followed.

The moment we pushed through the bar's door and into the open air, the cold slapped us like it knew what kind of night it had been. The heat and chaos of the dive bar vanished, replaced by sharp December air that stung against my cheeks and cut through the fabric of my coat.

I glanced down at my phone.

You just let me know when you need me to call.

All good. Solved itself.

Oh, this has got to be a good one.

Oh, it was. Maybe not good for my love life, but this one? It was gold for story time. Definitely the shortest date of the season so far. Eight minutes, maybe nine.

A new record.

Out of all of them, this one left me with a cocktail of emotions I hadn't expected. Angry. Appalled. Slightly amused.

Honestly, I didn't even know what I was feeling—but I was feeling a lot. My brain was still catching up.

I turned to see Cassie still standing behind me, phone in hand.

"Do you want to share a car?" she asked. "We can split it so you're not walking alone or anything. It's way too cold."

I blinked, surprised by the offer. "Yeah ... yeah, sure. Thanks."

It was too late for the metro anyway.

As we waited on the curb, she wrapped her scarf tighter and muttered, "God, this is why I don't go on dates anymore."

I let out a dry laugh. "I wish I could say the same."

"You go on a lot lately?"

I hesitated. "Kind of. I have this ... thing with some friends and friends of friends. A pact, sort of. Twelve blind dates before Christmas."

Cassie raised her eyebrows. "Twelve? You're kidding."

I shook my head.

"What date is this one?"

"Um, too many."

She whistled. "I wish you luck."

"Thanks." I was clearly going to need it.

"It's just wild to me that in the world, this is what we get? This is all that is available to us? I feel like by the time you hit thirty, it's all weirdos or married guys or guys who were married, which makes you wonder if they can handle a serious relationship again or if they are just a man child."

I laughed.

"It's not that funny."

"I know it isn't." I took a breath. "I'm laughing so that I don't cry."

"Oh," said Cassie, giving a small giggle herself. "All right then.

I'll take it. It's times like this I wonder if I should have just stayed with my high-school boyfriend, gotten knocked up, and called the rest a wash. At least I wouldn't be going through all this."

"I get that."

"But I had to girl-boss a little too close to the sun." She shook her head at herself.

"That's where we differ then," I said.

"You made it to the city looks like."

"Yeah, but..." She waited patiently. "I feel like I'm doing it all wrong."

"I doubt that," she smiled.

"I don't know. Are you living your childhood best friend and her brother who's been crashing on the couch for the past three months?" Or was it four now?

"Sounds like the start of a sitcom."

"Might as well be. Especially considering him being there is just..."

"You have a thing with him?"

"What?" I snapped my attention to look at her in the eyes as she raised her eyebrows expectantly. "No. No. It's not like that. It's just that I haven't seen him since we were kids. It's the job hunting that's been the hardest part since I got here."

"Ah."

"Yeah. I think that's partially why I'm going on all these stupid dates. Figured maybe if I had a guy by the end of the year maybe I wouldn't have to call the move a complete wash?" I said, feeling my cheeks heat. It was oddly embarrassing to admit out loud.

"What do you do?" Cassie asked.

"I'm a writer."

"Wow."

"I know."

"No," she quickly corrected. "I'm sorry. I didn't mean like *wow that's a terrible thing* or anything. I mean it. It's brave."

"I'm just ... trying to find a job. Any job at this point. Not even the bookstores are hiring. It feels like everywhere is either swamped or frozen for the holidays."

Cassie nodded knowingly as the car pulled up in front of us that Cassie ordered on her phone. She slid in first confirming our locations with the driver as I got situated next to her, barely managing to buckle my seatbelt before the car began to drive.

"It's brutal out there," she said, continuing our conversation. "Not to mention the job market goes full coma mode in December. But are you freelancing? Yeah? That still counts. A few of my friends are stringing together enough gigs to basically make a life out of it. Don't give up, okay?"

I took a breath, letting her words settle in a little. "Trying not to. I think the only thing holding me together at this point is living with my best friend, who badgered me to turn this entire mess into a newsletter."

Cassie's brows shot up. "This mess? You mean the twelve blind dates?"

I winced, laughing despite myself. "Yeah. That's the one."

"That's kind of genius."

"I'll probably delete them all as soon as it's over. I don't need my dating disaster arc living online forever, especially if none of it works out."

Cassie gave me a crooked smile. "Sometimes, you can make a happy ending out of anything, even the messiest start. Or at least something satisfying enough to keep going. Sorry, editorial brain kicking in. I don't write books, but I've built a career picking them apart and fangirling over the broken ones."

That made me smile. A real smile. "No, I actually like that. A lot."

Cassie leaned back in the seat with a grin. "Well, maybe you should get together with your best friend's brother you're living with?"

"Ha."

"I'm serious. Maybe it is just me, but a minute ago when you just talked about him... sounds like there is a bit of history there. Forgive me if I'm wrong."

Was I that obvious? "That would open up a whole other can of drama."

"Sure, but, come on. That would be a great story."

As the car slowed in front of my building, I pulled my bag onto my shoulder and reached inside for my wallet.

"I can send you my half over an app or—"

She waved me off. "Nah, don't worry about it."

"Thanks. Really."

Cassie turned slightly in her seat, her voice softer now. "Thanks for listening to me rant and saving me from that dude. If you hadn't walked in, I probably would've made excuses for him all night."

"Anytime," I said sincerely.

"Well, maybe I'll see you around, Brielle. And if not, definitely let me know if I make the cut in next week's edition," she said with a wink. "This ride was better than half the real dates I've had in years."

"Honestly?" I smiled. "Same here."

She opened her door, the cold rushing in again. "Happy holidays."

"Happy holidays," I said, stepping out into the night.

thirteen

I BREATHED IN THE WARM, lavender-scented steam. It curled up around my cheeks, fogging the edges of my thoughts like I was slowly, willingly cooking myself alive.

From the doorway, Gina let out a low whistle. "Oh my God. This looks like it was a bad one."

I didn't even lift my head. "I'm not sure if I'm still on the date or if this is the afterlife."

"Definitely the afterlife."

"Really?"

"I brought more cheap wine."

My lips curled up at the corners. "Heaven."

It didn't take long before Gina moved into full recovery mode—hair up, sleeves rolled, refilling the tub I was lounging in with more hot water, like she was tending a cauldron. She placed a glass of cheap rosé on the ledge next to me and plopped herself down on the floor beside the tub with her own feet kicked up on the closed lid of the toilet.

It was, objectively, the best bath I'd had in ages. And yet, even with the lavender bubbles and the gentle flicker of the emergency candle she insisted we light instead of turning on the fluorescent overhead, it just wasn't the right mood.

I couldn't shake the sticky nausea that still clung to me from earlier.

"He took a sip of my drink," I muttered, head falling dramatically into my hands after I recounted the dive situation.

Gina blinked. "Wait, what?"

"Before I took a sip."

"No way."

"To tell me that it wasn't poisoned."

Her face contorted in horrified disbelief. "You're making that up."

"I wish I were. That was his idea of charming."

Gina shuddered. "Oh my God. Was he wearing one of those plaid shirts that look like a dish towel?"

"Yes! I'm pretty sure he thought it was festive because it was red, sort of. And I swear he had an unusual amount of dirt under his nails."

She groaned so hard that I half expected her to throw her wineglass. "He didn't."

"He did." I buried my face in a washcloth. "I feel grimy."

Gina leaned over and dramatically sniffed the air above me. "You smell like a holistic skin-care store threw up in here, so we're making progress."

She slid back down, resting her head against her hand on the edge of the tub. "All right, so tonight was a mess, but the next one will be better."

I tilted my head to look at her. "You think?"

"I know it."

"I don't know." I sighed. "Maybe I should just give up here and now."

"Nah." She raised her glass and tapped it gently against the side of the tub. "You already have the next one planned for tomorrow, don't you?"

I nodded.

"Look at you. Getting out of your comfort zone. You can't give up now," encouraged Gina. "To the next. May he have clean fingernails and a basic understanding of manners."

"I'll take that. And maybe a Jingle Bell Martini."

"A what?"

I forgot I never told her about the details of my and Josh's practice date.

I shook my head. "I'm becoming delusional."

"And your standards are dropping fast."

"Just give me a man who doesn't treat dating like a group project on a deadline."

"That's fair."

I dropped deeper into the hot water until my shoulders floated. "Brighten my day then. Please. Tell me about your life. What's happening with this holiday show you've been buzzing about? I haven't had any new updates in a while."

Her eyes lit up instantly, her lips quirking around the rim of her glass. "The artist came in last night to start setting up. It's going to be all about light. There will be reflections, projections, mirrored panels, everything. Completely immersive."

"Sounds brilliant."

"That's literally the title!" she squealed, nearly sloshing her drink into the tub with me. "*Brilliance*."

THE
DATES TILL CHRISTMAS

BY BRIELLE THOMPSON

DATE FIVE

Location: A grungy, yet packed dive bar with one sad string of off-brand twinkle lights.
First Impression: He wore a red flannel that looked more like a dish cloth but I figured that he was just trying to be festive.

Ok. Let's get to the chance on this one. I get all dressed up and didn't get stood up. In fact, neither of us did. But guess who else was there at our date location?

A second woman. Also on a date with Date Five!

That's right. We were both there thinking we were on solo dates with this human raccoon, until he literally introduced us like it was no big deal. (After, let me add, he took a large sip of my drink directly from the straw to "test it was safe" *WHAT?*)

We both left. Date number two (or was I the other woman?) out with date number five and I. We shared a car and trauma-bonded for about 20 minutes until I arrived home.

I don't know what Date Five up to now. Probably giving someone else a UTI just by proximity.

But me? I went home. Brushed my teeth twice.

And tried not to think too hard about the suspiciously cloudy glass my vodka cran came in.

Blind Date Status: Date Five: 0 stars, but five stars for my new almost-girlfriend.

fourteen

AFTER LAST NIGHT'S disaster of a date, for some reason, date number five felt like date five hundred. At some point in the past few hours, a new sort of understanding that I was now a seasoned blind-date veteran sank in.

I was definitely getting less nervous each time I set up a new one. And more excited that I was officially well over the halfway point of this dating experiment I had let myself be conned into.

I managed to snag a small corner table in the bustling coffee shop. It was still slightly dark out as the sun started to pool through the wide front window. The workers behind the counter were like a well-oiled machine with each rush of hot air from the espresso machine to addressing people tapping their toes while waiting for their morning pick-me-up.

"Hot chocolate for Carol! Extra whip."

"A warmed cardamom bun for Ashlyn!"

Baristas called orders one after another as customers headed in and out of the door, which was coated in a gentle sweep of fog and condensation.

I lifted the lid of my laptop open, a half-empty cup of black coffee beside it. It was early—barely eight thirty a.m.—but the place was already buzzing with people ordering their morning fix before heading off to work, which made me feel like I was kind of doing the same thing right along with them.

I figured I might as well clean myself up after last night's disaster date at the dive bar and arrive for this one early so I could start the day off well, however date number six was going to go. If he showed up considering there was only a few minutes until our planned meeting time. Plus, I actually had a few writing jobs that had come through the other day that I needed to finish by the end of the week.

Though still, no full-time positions had magically pinged in my email.

It just made no sense. I was smart and practiced. I had a master's degree, for God's sake!

What else do these people want?

I had done everything I was supposed to do! Even if, yes, I could've chosen a more normal major with more job options, I now realized. Did I need to attach a song and jig to my next application, begging them to hire me?

At the very least, I was certain it would help me stand out.

My fingers, lightly covered with powdered sugar from the pastry I couldn't deny myself while I had been in line, hovered over the keyboard. I stared at my screen, squinting at the headline for my latest article. At first, I had thought the job was a scam. But, nope, it was real. A website wanted someone to write an article about lawn furniture.

And that someone was now me.

I stared at the untouched "Five Tips to Make Your Lawn Furniture Last Longer."

The title alone was making me feel like I was writing the world's least inspiring piece.

Have I really stooped this low?

I had thought maybe after that fun website gig I'd had from before, things might be looking up. This said otherwise. I kept writing, trying to watch as I hit the word count requirement.

But freelancing was a grind, and I needed the money. Between this, a few articles for lifestyle blogs, and some copy for a local restaurant's website, I was scraping by fine enough. Still, I'd gone to school for writing. Studied it. Practiced it. Did it for free for the sake of exposure. I didn't want to be typing about plastic chairs and Adirondack sets for the rest of my life.

My phone buzzed in my bag. It was Gina.

> I was just told he's running a little late, but he'll be there soon! He's cute though! Promise!

My eyes drifted over to the door of the café, as if I expected to see him walking in right at that moment.

To be honest, I didn't care as much as I probably should have, mainly because I didn't have high hopes. After a string of disappointing blind dates, my expectations were about as low as they could go at this point.

As if my never-ending job search wasn't keeping me humble enough.

And he's cute, huh? I thought skeptically. I'd heard that one before.

At exactly nine a.m., the door chimed, and a man in a sharp business suit entered. He was tall with short, dark hair and a confident air about him that immediately caught my attention. He looked like someone who had his life together—way more than I could say for myself, honestly.

He was scanning the room, probably looking for me.

Well, at least he doesn't look like a serial killer.

Standing up, I waved. After taking a second, he moved toward me with a smile I could only describe as warm.

"Hi. You're Brielle?"

"That's me," I agreed, shaking the hand he'd offered. No awkward hugs—thank God.

"Great. I'm Johnathan. John works," he said. "Sorry I'm late. I should be used to it around here by now, but traffic was a nightmare."

"No worries." I settled back into my seat, extending a hand toward the empty one across from me. "I was just getting some work done."

"Oh, that's great."

As he sat down, I noticed just how put together he was, unbuttoning his suit jacket.

He looked like he'd just walked out of a magazine ad for successful business people or maybe a high-end cologne commercial. I'd genuinely mentally prepared myself for a guy in a faded band tee and cargo shorts in winter because he wasn't going to let the weather control his *style*, like date number four ... or was that five?

I was getting them mixed up now.

But this guy? He was a complete surprise.

"So, how's your morning going?" John asked, adjusting his suit jacket and leaning in slightly.

I smiled, feeling a little more at ease than I had felt a bit ago, thinking about this eight hundredth date. "Pretty good actually. Like I said, I'm just getting some work done. It's nice to write outside of the house or else I turn into a troll, all holed up in my apartment until my roommate, Gina, insists I get out for some fresh air."

"You get into the zone."

I wished I could say yes, peeking back down at my ... article I was currently finishing up. "I'm a freelance writer, so my schedule is a little more flexible these days."

He raised a groomed eyebrow. "Oh."

"Something the matter?"

"No. That sounds interesting."

"Why do I think that isn't true."

"I'm sorry. It is." He shook his head, trying to get back on track. "What do you write, specifically?"

"Well …" I hesitated. Warning bells that something was about to go wrong started a gentle trill in the back of my mind. I'd had them built in between date three and four. Or was that a PTSD symptom? Post-traumatic stressful dates? "Mostly content for different brands. Like copywriting and articles for websites and stuff. Right now, I'm working on an article about lawn furniture."

John chuckled, and for a brief second, I thought he might've just been surprised or maybe trying to keep the conversation light. It was funny in a laugh or cry kind of way.

But then his face shifted into something more … amused and not at just the topic, but …

"Lawn furniture?" he repeated, clearly trying to hold back a laugh. "Wow, that's, uh … pretty specific."

"It is," I attempted to joke. "Isn't it?"

You know, it kind of sounds like one of those *starving artist* things. You know, where you're doing something completely unrelated to your dream job just to make ends meet."

I blinked, a bit stunned. I wasn't sure if he was teasing or if he really thought my work wasn't serious.

Though it was lawn furniture— No.

"Excuse me?" I asked, my tone a little sharper than I'd intended and my voice shaky. "I mean, I get that it's not the most glamorous topic, but it's still writing. And the pay isn't bad. It keeps me afloat while I search for more stable work."

John looked at me then—really looked at me—and his face immediately flushed with embarrassment. "Wait … you're serious?" He paused, then quickly said, "Sorry, I didn't mean to—I wasn't—I mean, that's actually really impressive. It's just … okay, lawn furniture? I didn't expect that."

I felt a wave of frustration building.

I could get up and leave, but this was a good seat. I had free coffee refills for at least another hour, and I didn't want to leave yet if not because I was hoping the date was going to go well, at least to get some work done for the day. For me.

And for right now, whether he thought it was worthwhile or not, writing was writing, and it paid the bills. Most of them, anyway. Now, here he was, a guy who seemed to have every-thing figured out, treating my work like it was a joke.

I could make fun of myself. God, I could even be downright critical. But I wasn't going to let this guy do it for me.

"I guess I'm just doing what I can right now," I said, trying to mask my irritation. "It's not always glamorous, but it's work. And I'm trying to get my foot in the door with bigger projects."

John's expression softened, and he leaned back, looking sheepish. "I'm sorry. I didn't mean to offend you. It's just … well, I guess I was expecting something more. I don't know."

I waited.

"I figured my friends who set us up knew my type by now."

Like how I was now figuring out he certainly wasn't my type—corporate douche.

"All right then," I muttered, taking a deep breath.

"I just like someone who is put-together and knowing what they're doing with their lives at this point—you understand?" His ears flushed as if he was now hearing what he was saying. He quickly started to backpedal. "I didn't mean it like that. Really. I respect the hustle. You're just not what I was expecting."

There was a long, uncomfortable silence before I trusted myself to speak again. "It's been nice meeting you, John. I'll let our mutual know that it just didn't work out, though I appreciate them trying since, externally, you're very cute. Internally? Ick."

He startled, like I might as well have wrinkled my nose and held an *X* out in front of my body to ward him away from me.

"That way, they won't get your *type* wrong again. But I think you should probably get going so I can get back to work," I said. "I'm very dedicated to my work after all, even if you don't see it that way."

"I didn't—yeah, of course," he said quickly, standing. "I'm really sorry about what happened before. I didn't mean to meet you like that. God, I sound like a complete ass."

He chuckled. I was glad someone was having a good time.

I raised my eyebrows at him. He didn't notice for another minute. Strike that. More like a minute and a half.

"I guess we just aren't a good fit. I can get you another coffee to make up for my rudeness, if you'd like."

I forced myself to smile tightly. "It's fine. Thanks though. Have a good day."

He nodded, looking genuinely apologetic.

I watched as he walked toward the door. Oddly enough, though I'd had such little expectations, I'd still managed to feel more than a little deflated. Another hopefully promising start, but in the end, it felt like yet another reminder that I was on the outside of what most people considered "real" work.

At this point, I wasn't sure I'd ever get to "real" work status.

Pressing my lips together, I glanced toward my tabs at the top of my computer screen and opened up the one farthest to the right. There were a few new comments on my newest newsletter.

Opening up another page, I smirked. At least I didn't have to write about lawn furniture now. I had another plain coffee. However, by the time I hit the bottom of the cup, my stomach started to churn.

I reached down to hold my stomach as the room started to swirl with the sound of the espresso machine.

Whether it was the second bad date in twenty-four hours or too much caffeine, I was no longer feeling ready to take on the day.

fifteen

THERE WAS no way that I was finishing my next newsletter, let alone any more lawn furniture assignments. I needed to get home.

Beads of sweat started to accumulate under my loose bangs. Had the coffee shop turned up the heat? My hair stuck to my skin as I fanned myself with a hand. Another laptop worker next to me curled her lip in disgust at me, wearing her oversize turtleneck, as cool as can be.

I quickly started to pack my things, knocking my hip into her small bistro table.

"Sorry," I murmured.

I thought she might've said something in response, like, "Watch where you are going," but I wasn't paying attention.

I tore past a laughing couple and out onto the sidewalk.

The crisp morning had been replaced with a thick coldness in the air that made the fact that I could feel sweat on my skin even worse. I didn't think I was getting sick, but something definitely wasn't right.

By the time I made it through the apartment door, letting it slam behind me as I dropped my tote bag, laptop inside, against the wall. I sagged against the wall with relief.

Made it.

The question now was, what was I supposed to do? Was I going to faint? Or lose my coffee breakfast?

I really should've stopped after that second cup. I was being punished now by the coffee gods, wasn't I?

I tugged at the neck of my coat, then pulled down the zipper, which got caught on the edge of the fabric that was meant to keep the wind off of me, though right now, it felt like a straitjacket.

"Come on," I moaned, yanking at the zipper.

At that moment, my stomach rolled high up into my ribs, along with another wave of hot nausea.

Yep. I was definitely going to be sick.

At least no one was here to see it. I just needed to make it to the bathroom. I took a step, most of my weight still leaning against the wall.

I didn't hear the door open behind me until it shut, startling me another step forward as I twisted around. My body didn't appreciate the abrupt movement.

Josh stood in front of me, looking me over as his eyes widened. Easily, without the struggle I was having, he unzipped his coat. He slung it over one of the hooks. "Brielle? You don't look good."

"Wow," I choked out. I tried to force myself to sound easy-breezy, like there was no problem at all. Even though my entire body felt anything but easy-breezy and there definitely was a problem. "Thanks."

He shook his head, taking a step toward me.

I blinked at him. "You should be at work."

"I came home early. I had an appointment."

"Oh, that's good. Half days are nice. You already have those saved up when you just started?"

"They allow sick days for appointments."

I nodded, feeling another wave of nausea. I sucked my cheeks in, trying to quell it as I leaned over my knees.

"Is something the matter? You don't look good. You're clearly sick."

I couldn't answer. I needed to get to the bathroom. Now. Thirty seconds ago. Five minutes ago so that I could turn the lock and get on my knees in front of the toilet before Josh walked in the door. But it was too late.

"Brielle, are you okay?"

I was ... fine.

I was great.

"Fantastic," I said.

And then I threw up all over his shoes.

sixteen

SECRETLY, I hoped that sleazy Jackson from his not-holiday dive bar was also throwing his guts up if this was from the bar. Even though, for some reason, I had a feeling that he was likely still living it up with his two-dates-a-night schedule. That grimy bar was probably his breeding ground. He was immune to the layer of grime on the glassware.

I was pretty sure I was actually suffering from a very real case of food poisoning. Glass poisoning? It seemed odd that it had taken this long to settle in, but ...

At least I hadn't been drugged.

I almost wanted to laugh—if I didn't want to cry at how nauseous I felt.

I told Josh about the whole tasting my drink for drugs bit that Jackson did, though he didn't think it was quite as funny as I did now looking back.

"What an asshole."

"I already went over this with Gina."

"Well, I agree with you both," he said.

That made me feel somewhat validated. Even as I sat next to the toilet with my hair stuck to my forehead. Validation quickly returned to embarrassment as Josh squatted down next to me and—God—flushed the toilet. Again.

I shut my eyes in shame.

"You done?" he asked.

"I think so."

"You might just have a virus."

"But that feels so much less fun to say than I was actually poisoned environmentally by another bad date. The readers would get a kick out of it."

He chuckled. "Readers?"

"Kind of. Online."

"You're writing again?"

I wiped beneath my eyes and checked my fingers. Mascara. Of course.

"It's silly," I muttered.

"I doubt that," he said. "Unless you're writing comedy. Then it's probably hysterical."

"Well, I guess it kind of is then. Gina talked me into starting a newsletter, and my life might as well be a joke these days."

I gave him a half-hearted smile.

"It's mostly just for me. Misery loves company and all that, so at least it feels like I'm not writing to an empty room."

"Are all the dates really going that bad?" he asked, settling into the corner cushion, one arm slung lazily over the back.

I huffed. "If I say yes, will it make me sound like I'm the problem?"

"Doubtful."

"I've had six dates," I said, wincing. "And I think I have another one tonight—which, right now, just makes me want to curl up and die."

"Oof."

I exhaled. "And there are still so many more left. I don't know how I'm supposed to pull off twelve before Christmas."

"Why do you keep doing it then?"

I blinked. "What do you mean?"

"I mean," he said with a slight shrug, as if what he was about to say was completely obvious, "you could just ... stop going on the blind dates."

I stared at him. It was such a simple thing to say. So logical. And I had thought about it. But saying no would mean letting someone down. Gina who went to all the trouble along with her friends to set me up. Maybe, even a bit, me.

It would mean stopping the momentum when everything else in my life already felt stalled.

"I don't want to disappoint Gina," I said finally, my voice quieter than I'd expected.

"She'll get over it," he said, and there was a softness in his tone, not dismissive, but understanding. "She's barely home anyway."

"I know. But she's excited about it. And lately, I guess..." I gave a nervous laugh, immediately wishing I hadn't said that much. "It's stupid."

Josh didn't laugh. He just waited.

"Things have changed, you know? Even though it feels easy again—living with her, talking like old times—we've grown up. It's not the same anymore. So, this gives us a thing. A grounding point."

His hummed as he took in my response. "I get that."

I looked at him—really looked. His hair was tousled, hoodie wrinkled. He was a lot like the guy I remembered years ago, but different. Comfortable in a way that made the conversation even more easy. Neither of us hiding who we were from each other like on all these dates I was going on. I was so used to having to put my best foot forward. Here, with him. I could just be.

Even if right now I was being sick on the bathroom floor.

"These guys you're going on these dates with," he said, rubbing a hand along his jaw, "they're really screwing it up out there, huh?"

"Apparently." I gave him a sideways glance. "Are you dating right now?" The words were out before I could stop them. I wanted to claw them back immediately.

Josh paused, and something unreadable passed over his face. His fingers flexed against his leg.

"Nope," he said finally.

I didn't realize I'd been holding my breath until I let it go. Though I shouldn't have been feeling what I did. Relief.

"You should," I said after a second.

His brow lifted. "Should what?"

"Date," I said carefully. "You're a catch, right? Isn't that what guys like you always say?"

He grunted as he pushed up off the floor, stretching his arms behind his back. "You trying to put me through the same sort of torture you are?"

I laughed, tilting my head back and letting my eyes drift closed. "Just suggesting."

Josh stood for a moment, quiet. Then, before walking past, he ruffled the top of my head lightly—like I was still the girl who used to tag along behind him and Gina in the summer heat.

But I wasn't her anymore.

And I had a feeling he knew that too.

"How about I help you get up off the floor?" he offered. "How are you feeling?"

"Oddly better."

He shrugged. "That's a good sign."

"I guess so."

"Just get some rest and see how you're feeling later."

I nodded, letting my body weight lean against him as he

walked me next door to my room. This was becoming a habit. Yet he didn't make a complaint as he pulled back the blanket on my bed and maneuvered me until I was sitting on the edge.

"In." He directed my legs.

"Thank you."

Shaking his head, he walked toward the blinds and shut them until we were in near darkness. "I'll get you some water."

"Can you get me my bag too? I dropped it by the door. I wasn't finished with my computer."

Pausing, Josh looked at me again. Though I felt a little better, I guess I still wasn't looking well enough for a computer. He nodded anyway.

"Thank you," I repeated, watching him turn toward the door.

I let my head loll to the side on my pillow as my eyes followed his long steps out the door and into the quiet apartment, where I heard the cabinet open and a glass being filled with water from the tap.

I was asleep before he got back.

THE
12 DATES TILL CHRISTMAS

BY BRIELLE THOMPSON

DATE SIX

Location: Coffee shop.
First Impression: Late, but I can't help it, some men just look amazing in a suit.

Date Six was supposed to be low-key. A cozy coffee shop. He showed up a little late but otherwise looked... so much better than prior blind dates already.

But then it happened. The Moment.

If you're a creative, you know the one. He asked what I did for work, and I said "freelance writing," and he blinked so hard I thought he was having a mental crisis.

Then he said, "Wait ... you're serious?"

Sir. SIR.

I'm figuring things out. I'm writing this newsletter you're not subscribed to! I am paying taxes! I am 90% caffeine and hope at this point.

Anyway, that was it, basically. A very much non-starter sort of date. I didn't force it into anything else. Just when he left to let me get back to work on my own for the rest of the morning my stomach — already suspicious after Date Five's questionable glassware — staged a rebellion.

Gathering my stuff, I headed home. I didn't even get a chance to say anything to my best friend's brother who was there before I threw up directly on his shoes.

Blind Date Status: I think that last line about says it all.

seventeen

THE SCENT of warm coffee and maybe cinnamon hung in the air as I opened my bedroom door. The living room was quiet, except for the low hum of music from someone's phone.

I shuffled into the kitchen like a ghost freshly risen from the grave, hair a mess, wearing the same sweatshirt I'd thrown on sometime after waking up. I'd huddled in the bathroom again and then dragged myself out for the final time at around two a.m.

Josh stood by the counter in soft joggers and a henley with sleeves pushed to his elbows, pouring a glass of water with the kind of casual grace that made my half-dead body feel personally offended.

"Hey," he said, looking up when he noticed me. "How are you feeling?"

"Oddly ... fine." My voice came out hoarse, a surprise even to me.

He walked over and held out the glass. "That's a relief. I was ready to call an ambulance if you didn't move by noon."

"Thank you," I murmured, taking the water. My fingers

brushed his, and I tried not to think about it too hard. "Gina left already?"

"Headed out a few hours ago."

I remembered, at one point last night, she had gently knocked on the bathroom door to check on me, though I wasn't one for much conversation at the time. She mentioned something about having someone curse Jackson.

I hadn't told her not to.

He leaned back against the counter, arms crossed, watching me as I slowly sipped.

"Once you get changed," he said casually, "and finish your water, I have a question for you."

Unable to stall anymore, the glass empty, I looked at him. "Should I be concerned?"

"Only if you hate fun." He tilted his head toward the stove clock. "If you're up for it, that is."

I narrowed my eyes. "Define *up for it.*"

"Ever heard of speed-wrapping holiday gifts?"

I blinked at him. "Speed ... wrap?"

He gave a sheepish grin. "Okay, so that's not technically the official name. But from what I hear, that's what it turns into after the first ten minutes."

"So, you've never done this before?"

"No, but it counts as one of my evening extracurriculars that I'm supposed to check off before the school year ends. I'm two behind."

I gasped in mock betrayal and lightly swatted the back of his arm. "You're using me to score teacher points?"

"Absolutely not." His grin widened. "I'm using you to win the totally unofficial—and very serious—gift-wrapping face-off at the school's holiday fundraiser."

I stared at him, partially amused, even more skeptical.

"If you were still sick," he added, "I might have sweetened the deal with rumors of a cookie exchange and hot chocolate bar."

I rolled my eyes dramatically. "Now you're just playing dirty."

He shrugged. "I prefer the term *strategic incentive deployment*."

I leaned against the fridge, pretending to consider it. "You just said it wasn't a competition."

"It's not." He paused. "Not really."

"Josh."

He grinned. "Fine. But between you and me, I still bet I can wrap more presents than you during our shift."

I took another sip of water and narrowed my eyes at him. "That sounds like a challenge."

"It is."

"Then you're on."

* * *

I tugged off my scarf as we climbed the stone steps up to the school's main entrance. The brick building was decked out with string lights and makeshift cardboard snowflakes taped to the windows.

Through the glass, I could already hear laughter echoing from the gym and smell something dangerously sugary in the air.

Josh swiped his school badge that had a picture of him that made him look like a mad scientist. Why in the world had his hair looked like that on picture day? I didn't think I'd ever seen him use hair gel in his life.

Had it been a bet? A dare?

He held the door open for me. "Prepare yourself."

"For?"

"Holiday madness. Kids hyped up on candy canes and divorced dads pretending they know how to use Scotch tape."

"You really know how to paint a picture."

The second we stepped inside, I was hit by warmth, bright lighting, and the unmistakable chaos of a school holiday fundraiser. Long folding tables were piled with unwrapped donations. Parents bustled about in red sweaters. And there, at the end of the room, was a whiteboard labeled *Wrapping Wars* with tally marks already in progress.

It was hard not to think that you weren't a holiday extraordinaire from the moment you walked into the middle school, however. The entire gym had been transformed into a sort of wonderland that represented any winter holiday the kids celebrated.

Classic tunes circulated through the speakers. Armed with colorful rolls of wrapping paper, shiny ribbons, and an assortment of gift tags, staff cleared a space on foldable white tables. It transformed the gym into a wrapping headquarters.

I guessed that made us holiday elves. With Josh's bright burgundy hat that was a size too large for his head with a giant white puff ball on top, the elf metaphor felt even more apt.

On one side of the gym, there were parents helping their kids wrap their cheap plastic trinkets they had purchased at the school's Christmas market.

Josh and I, along with a half dozen others, were on toy donations that would be going to the local shelter brought in throughout the month before the holidays so that those who stayed there would have something to open the day of Christmas when everyone else was looking beneath a tree for what Santa might've brought them.

* * *

I dropped the next gift onto the center of a bright red sheet of wrapping paper. I looked over the doll, complete with a hairbrush and a change of clothing including a pink dress and matching plastic purse, mentally calculating just how much paper I was going to need. I sliced through the paper confidently in one crisp swipe.

I had never speed-wrapped presents before, and now I honestly thought it should be considered an Olympic sport. Or at least a holiday sport. Was there such a thing?

The DIY television channel or the local Home Haven magazine would eat this kind of thing up.

Maybe I could attempt to pitch Home Haven again as their website started to publish more. Get in before other writers got wind of just how much charity one of the smaller middle schools was doing in the city.

"Now you're getting the hang of it," Josh commented, slapping a bow perfectly straight on the top of his latest box, which looked like some kind of building block set. "Soon enough, you'll be wrapping yours at a fast pace."

"Ha-ha," I said blandly, though he was already moving on to the next gift.

I quickly shifted my attention back to what I was doing. I started to twist the present around and find a rhythm that Josh had already seemed to perfect. The paper hugged the box gently before I taped the seams, though I still had an odd bump on one edge.

Was it from too much paper? Or had I just not tucked it correctly?

I glanced toward Josh to see if he noticed my struggle before I reached for a shiny gold bow to stick on top, hoping that it detracted from my awkward wrapping job.

I passed along a rectangular box wrapped in cartoon snowmen before being handed another gift to wrap. This one was smaller—jewelry-sized. I didn't open it, but I let myself imagine a tiny ballerina spinning inside the box as I reached for the yellow polka-dot paper from the pile.

"People at the school actually donated all of these toys?" I asked.

Josh nodded, his hands moving with practiced ease as he sliced clean lines into a sheet of red foil paper. "Yeah. They've got a solid community here and have been doing this for a few years now. They have a sort of tree that parents or local businesses even, can take a tag off of. Each tag shares different toys or gifts that families at the shelter need." He paused to crease a crisp fold. "I heard this haul is nearly double what they collected last year."

I looked down at the growing mountain of wrapped gifts with a new sort of appreciation. "That's kind of amazing. I didn't realize people around here were so intense about Christmas."

"The school district here takes its holiday spirit seriously."

"You like it here?" I asked instead, my voice quiet but curious.

Josh cocked his head slightly, the corners of his mouth lifting, like he was trying to decide if I was being serious.

"Yeah," he said after a second. "I like it here. The school's good. Kids are good. It's not forever, but ... for now? I'm happy." He gave a small shrug, as if that was the best explanation he could offer.

And maybe it was.

We kept folding and taping in companionable silence, the buzz of the fundraiser filling the space around us. Kids squealed as they rushed to pick their wrapped presents from the Winter Wishes table. A dad with a glitter beard tried—and failed—to stuff a basketball into a square gift box. Laughter floated through the air, mingled with the soft sounds of Mariah Carey and the scent of sugar cookies warming in foil trays.

Wrapping was something I usually did while half watching a holiday movie on my own, but now it had somehow turned into something fun. Especially when I glanced over and saw Josh crouching beside a little girl in a fuzzy antler headband, asking her what her favorite part of the event was.

Her answer was, "Cookies and coloring," and his laugh—warm, soft, real—made something in my stomach flip.

Something about seeing him here—so naturally himself, so good with people—made the ache of disappointment from my never-ending string of horrible dates feel more distant than it had been sneaking up on me again. How couldn't it? I mean, after a while whether it be two dates of six now, it was hard not to think that things weren't working out because, well, me.

By the time our shift ended, we had a stack of shiny, haphazardly labeled gifts towering beside the main tree and only one minor paper-cut injury between us.

Josh looked a little too pleased with himself.

"What?"

"You don't have to say anything. I know I won," he said with that insufferably smug grin.

I rolled my eyes, though a smile tugged at the corners of my mouth. "You knew you were going to win."

"Confidence is key," he said, tossing a ribbon spool into the bin like it was a basketball.

"And here I was, thinking this was about giving back to your new school community."

"Oh, it is." He leaned in a little, voice dropping conspiratorially. "But it's also about crushing your opponents with speed, precision, and superior tape control."

I let out a laugh I hadn't expected. "You're unbelievable."

"And yet," he said with a wink, "you still agreed to team up with me."

I rolled my eyes again. "Yeah, well … I was sick. My judgment was compromised."

He grinned. "No take-backs."

* * *

As we stood by the exit, coats in hand and breath fogging lightly in the crisp December air that seeped through the school's old double doors, I could already feel my body beginning to drag. My fingers were sore from folding and taping, and I had a glitter smear on my wrist from some rogue ribbon that had clearly fought back.

Josh glanced at the time on his phone and then at me. "You're still going on that date tonight?"

I groaned. Out loud. "Unfortunately."

He raised an eyebrow at my dramatics, bursting with one of his laughs. "You don't sound very excited."

"That's because I'm not." I hugged my coat to my chest without putting it on yet. "This was supposed to be a rest-and-recover day after being sick, not wrap four hundred presents, then go smile for two hours at another guy who talks about how he's totally different from other guys."

Josh smirked and held out a hand. "Here. Arms."

"What?"

"Come on. If I'm sending you into the dating war zone, the least I can do is make sure you're properly bundled."

Despite the eye roll I gave him, I let him take my coat and slid my arms into it. His hands were warm, his touch careful and grounding in a way that made my skin buzz beneath the fabric. He tugged the coat gently up around my shoulders, and then, without hesitation, he reached forward and pulled the zipper up for me.

His fingers brushed against my neck lightly as he adjusted the collar, shouldn't have made my heart flutter. But it did. Dammit.

"There," he said softly, like it wasn't a big deal. Like my pulse hadn't just picked up.

I managed to speak around the growing weight in my chest. "Thanks."

"You're welcome. Even if I still think you shouldn't go."

I looked up at him, our breath mingling in the small space between us. "What would I do instead? Stay in and watch a movie with you and eat leftover cookies?"

He didn't miss a beat. "Yes. You could also come with me. My friend invited me over to a small get-together. Just movies and stuff tonight. But they are probably better company than whatever weirdo you've got lined up."

Yeah. That sounded infinitely better than whatever awkward two-drink minimum was waiting for me across town.

But I'd already committed. And I didn't trust myself to know if staying in with Josh would be easier or harder.

"I promised Gina," I said finally.

"Forget about my sister."

"Don't be rude."

He huffed.

"And the guy seems normal. At least so far."

There was an unreadable shift in his expression. "Well ... if it goes bad, you know where to find me. I'll save you a snickerdoodle."

That earned him a small laugh from me. "Deal."

As we stepped out into the icy air, I found myself walking slower than usual, dragging my boots through a thin dusting of snow on the sidewalk, as if the date wouldn't happen if I just didn't move fast enough.

Josh walked beside me quietly, close enough that our arms brushed once or twice.

It was nothing.

eighteen

THE MESSAGE CAME ten minutes before I planned to leave.

> Need to cancel. Rain check if u wanna?

I stared at the message from what was supposed to be Date Seven for a full thirty seconds before my jaw ticked. *If I wanna?*

I huffed, thumbing out the most neutral, inoffensive response I could manage.

> Maybe another time. Have a happy holiday!

There. That was polite enough. Noncommittal.

I set my phone down on the coffee table and flopped back onto the couch like someone had pulled the strings from my spine. So much for the grand finale of this twelve-date experiment. What a way to close out a week of near-emotional whiplash, digestive sabotage, and existential dread with a side of seasonal depression.

Gina couldn't say I hadn't tried at least.

The apartment was quiet. Josh had gone to the gym a bit ago, and now the shower was running—steam already seeping out from the crack under the bathroom door. I picked up the remote, stared at it, and then remembered that I couldn't start the next episode without him. We had rules. Our show was sacred territory.

Instead, I let the remote bounce softly in my hands, back and forth, like it might suggest something else to do.

Maybe I'd finish the newsletter post I'd half written that morning, if I could get past the part where I admitted the only highlight of the day was wrapping-paper-related injuries.

The bathroom door creaked open just then, and Josh walked out, rubbing a towel through his damp hair as he moved toward the hall. He looked unfairly good. And not in his usual workout gear either. Loose, dark jeans. A clean, fitted shirt that looked like it had been chosen on purpose.

"You look nice," I said casually—or as close to it as I could get with my pulse doing a weird little double beat in my neck. "Aren't you heading out soon?"

Josh looked over, pausing mid-motion to ruffle his hair one last time with the towel. "Yeah. But what about you? Aren't you supposed to be leaving too?"

I lifted the remote like it held all the answers. "Change of plans."

He tilted his head, waiting.

"My date canceled," I explained, "ten minutes before I was supposed to leave."

His expression flickered. "You're kidding."

"Nope. Is it bad to say I'm kind of relieved?"

He laughed under his breath and leaned against the wall, folding his arms. "Honestly? No. You've had a full day. I probably pushed you too hard with the whole wrapping shift."

"Are you kidding? That was the most fun I've had in weeks,"

I said, smiling. "In fact, I'm pretty sure I could count speed-gift-wrapping as date number nine."

The joke hung there for a second too long before I noticed how still Josh had gotten, a tight look crossing his face.

"Not that I think it was a date," I rushed to clarify, my face heating. "Obviously."

Josh shrugged, but his eyes held mine in a way that felt suddenly ... less casual.

"Well," he said after a pause, shifting his weight off the wall, "since you're officially off duty tonight, you're welcome to come with me now."

"To ..."

"My friend's place," he said, running a hand through his hair, suddenly sheepish. "A few people from the school are getting together for some food and drinks. Nothing wild. Just a little holiday hangout. You'd fit right in. Plus, now that your night's free ..."

I blinked. "You want me to come with you?"

"I invited you, didn't I?" he said. "Like I said, we're just watching a Christmas movie or something. Other people will be there too. Don't sit here in the dark again, all because yet another flighty asshole bailed on you. Unless you're still not feeling better."

I considered the offer. I didn't feel too terrible anymore. If anything, sitting here, I felt restless. "What are we watching?"

"A classic, of course. What else?"

nineteen

"I WOULDN'T CALL *Die Hard* a classic."

Josh chuckled as he led me farther inside of his friend's apartment. I expected it to smell like the college apartments I had been in, but it oddly held the scent of cinnamon and air freshener.

"Depends who you ask, I guess."

"Yep," I said, rolling my eyes good-naturedly. "How could I miss *Die Hard* on Christmas?"

Josh's friend gave a wide smile. "You're in for a wild ride. Who needs a Christmas rom-com when you've got this? Hi. I'm Matt."

"Nice to meet you. I'm Brielle."

"Brielle! Good to have ya. I told Josh that he could bring someone around if he wanted to tonight. He keeps talking about you."

"Oh." I glanced at Josh. He didn't say anything. It was my turn, I guessed, to set the record straight much like Josh did our first night out at the bar when he ran into an old co-worker, even if the words felt stiff coming out. "Must not be me. We aren't together or anything. My friend—his sister is my friend, and now we live together, but just as friends."

Matt pressed his lips together and nodded. "I think I got it. Either way, glad to have you. *Mi casa es tu casa.* There are drinks in the fridge and snacks out."

"Thanks."

Once Matt headed to the kitchen to grab himself a drink, Josh stepped behind me, his hands brushing my shoulders as he helped slide off my coat. He'd done the same thing earlier, and just like before, the sensation lit a current of awareness down my spine. I told myself it was just the temperature difference between inside and out, but we both knew better.

As I turned slightly, he leaned in close, his breath grazing the shell of my ear. "You didn't have to do that."

I blinked, tilting my head to glance up at him. "Do what?"

"Tell Matt we weren't together." Josh's jaw shifted. He didn't quite meet my eyes.

"It's not a big deal," I said with a shrug, trying to downplay the weird tightness in my chest. "I just figured maybe you wanted that line drawn. Like at the bar, with your other friend the other week. I didn't want you to feel uncomfortable."

Josh gave a short nod. "All good."

But something in the way he'd said it told me it wasn't.

I didn't press.

We moved deeper into the apartment, which, in contrast to our shared space, felt freshly scrubbed and expensive. Wide windows spilled soft light across mid-century furniture, and I could see the blinking red of a water tank on a neighboring rooftop. A little oasis tucked into the city skyline.

A few of Josh's friends greeted us with nods and casual warmth. One of them practically melted into the couch with a girl snoozing on his shoulder.

"Nice to meet you, Brielle." They each offered a friendly smile.

"Nice to meet you too."

"How do you know Josh?"

"My sister," Josh answered quickly before I could open my mouth.

"That's cool. You new to the city or a repeat offender, like this guy?"

"I've been here a few months," I said, tucking my hands into the sleeves of my oversized cardigan sweater. "Still trying to find a job though."

"What do you do?"

"She's a writer," Josh said, quick, confident. Still not looking at me.

I glanced over at him.

"She's got a newsletter with a *solid* audience," he added.

I wouldn't say a solid audience. "It's new."

"That's awesome," the guy replied, impressed. "What kind of stuff do you write?"

"Mostly essays right now," I said. "Stories, I guess. It's a little bit of everything."

Josh settled onto the couch. I hesitated only briefly before slipping into the open spot beside him. The alternative was either perching awkwardly near a group of guys I didn't know or sitting on the floor. Not ideal options when my entire body still felt vaguely like a food poisoning hangover.

Besides, sitting next to Josh felt ... familiar. Safe. At least, that was what I told myself.

The movie had already started—*Die Hard*, of course. The undisputed king of holiday-adjacent action films.

The others chatted about sports and work, filling the space with easy conversation, but I was only half listening. Every time Josh shifted next to me, every accidental brush of his shoulder against mine, it sent little sparks ricocheting through my system.

I was a mess.

Get it together, I told myself. *It's just Josh. Couch dweller. Childhood fixture. Professional toast burner.*

He was Gina's brother. And I was definitely—*definitely*—not allowed to feel like this.

But then Matt, now back and settled across the couch, leaned toward me with a friendly grin.

"I really was surprised to see Josh bring someone," he said. "He's always collecting friends, but ..."

"I had other plans actually. He just saved me from a pretty pathetic night alone."

"Really? What happened?"

"My date canceled. It was last minute."

"What an idiot. Our gain," he said with an easy wink. "You made the better call anyway. *Die Hard* over overpriced tapas and weak cocktails? No contest."

That made me laugh. "You're not wrong."

We fell into a surprisingly comfortable rhythm. We talked about movies, mutual hatred of mall crowds this time of year, and how Christmas shopping got more competitive every year. It was easy in a way I hadn't expected. And it was ... kind of nice. A break from the awkwardness I'd been drowning in for weeks.

Josh, meanwhile, had stood and wandered off toward the kitchen. The open floor plan made it easy to see him from where I sat—his tall frame moving around the fridge and cabinets.

"Anyone need a snack?" he called over his shoulder.

"I'm good," Matt said, his gaze flicking back to me. "So, you like the city so far? Josh mentioned you were writing, but didn't say much more."

I started to respond, "Yeah—"

"Could you actually help me with something?" Josh interrupted, still near the fridge but looking directly at Matt now. His voice was polite, but there was a sharpness beneath it.

Matt looked at him, clearly confused. "Uh ... sure."

He stood, apologizing with a cheery smile. "Be right back."

I watched as he crossed to the kitchen. Josh didn't move until Matt was close, and then the two of them disappeared just out of sight, behind the edge of a cabinet.

The low hum of conversation filled the room, but I suddenly couldn't hear any of it. I stared straight ahead at the movie, but my pulse was thumping hard in my ears.

Josh hadn't looked at me once.

And I couldn't tell if it was because he was annoyed ... or jealous.

Or worse, if I wanted him to be.

Smiling, I leaned back into the couch as the movie continued, though it appeared we were almost already past the halfway point. I might not be a die-hard fan of *Die Hard*, like Matt was, but I was kind of sad it was going so quickly.

Matt came back with his lips pressed together, sitting down on the other end of the couch.

I raised my eyebrows at him as he situated himself to get more comfortable. "All good?"

"Great. Can't believe I missed so much of the movie."

"I was just thinking the same thing."

He gave a single curt nod.

I narrowed my eyes. "What did Josh need help with?"

He glanced at me. "Huh?"

Blinking, I couldn't help but feel a drastic shift in his demeanor.

What had just happened?

Matt had been easygoing and even playful with me a second ago, but now his attention was entirely focused on me, and there was something about his look that made my stomach churn.

Swallowing, I refocused my attention back on the television, and Matt turned his previously chatty energy back to his friends, who were talking about the differences between the uptown versus downtown restaurant they all liked.

Josh flopped back down on the couch beside me with a loud sigh, as if nothing had changed.

"Hey," I said, nudging him.

He crunched on a fistful of popcorn. He barely glanced at me out of the corner of his eye. "What?"

I breathed out through my nose and shook my head. I looked between him and then toward Matt again. He didn't seem to get the hint, and I ... didn't say anything.

Everyone quietly chatted like nothing had happened between the two of them when he mysteriously lured Matt away to the kitchen and returned with a personality transplant.

"Nothing."

"Good movie?" He asked.

"Great," I said, my voice tight.

twenty

BY THE TIME the movie was over, I was more than ready to head home. For a moment I had been energized and happy being out and not on a date. That was until Josh's nonplussed behavior along with erratic switch from interested to not interested signals Matt was giving showed up. Though, of course, Josh had nothing to do with that.

Of course not.

I barely spared Josh a glance on the way home. I wanted to be mad about whatever he must've said to Matt to make him stop talking to me so suddenly—since that had to be it! But, I was more confused than anything else. Why would he do that? I just didn't get it.

I slung my coat, scarf, and purse over the hallway hook, and the thing chose that exact moment to rip clean off the wall.

I stared down at the mess on the floor—coat, scarf, purse in a heap.

Perfect.

I didn't bother picking anything up. Just stepped over the whole disaster and kept walking.

I was done.

"Bri, wait," Josh called behind me, sounding tired.

I closed my eyes for a second before I turned around, forcing a smile. "What's up?"

Josh tilted his head a little, watching me. I waited for whatever it was he was about to say. "Don't look at me like that."

"Like what?" I asked, all wide-eyed innocence. "I'm not looking at you like anything."

He raised his eyebrows in that way he did when he was trying to call me out without saying a word. Usually, I rose to that challenge. Not tonight.

"I'm tired," I said honestly. "I'm heading to bed."

"Brielle." He scoffed.

He actually scoffed at me.

I stopped just shy of my bedroom door. My back stiffened.

"You can't be mad at me."

"I'm not mad at you," I said.

"It really feels like you are."

I shrugged. "I wonder why."

Josh hesitated. "So, you are."

I didn't say anything. I didn't have to.

"Matt ..." he started, then stopped.

I folded my arms. "Yes, Josh. Matt. What was that all about?"

"What was what about?"

I took a step toward my room.

"Can we talk?"

"You want to talk?" I turned back to face him. "Then tell me why Matt suddenly looked like he wanted to run a background check on me after we just had a perfectly normal conversation. A good one. Better than I'd had with anyone on these exhausting blind dates Gina had set me up with."

"You don't want to date Matt."

Was he serious? "That's not your decision to make."

"He's not ready to date someone like you."

"Oh, great." I gestured toward him. "Go on. Enlighten me. What's someone like me?"

Josh pressed his lips together, like he regretted even saying that much.

"Someone who's ... good," he finally said. "Someone who's strong and actually shows up. You give a damn about people. He doesn't. He can't even text a girl back, let alone—he's not going to be what you need, Brielle. He'd ruin it. And he'd ruin you."

My chest tightened. "All right. If that's true, then fine. But that still doesn't make it your place to step in. I don't need you to protect me. God, I'm not thirteen anymore."

"I know that."

"Then what did you say to him?"

Josh sighed. "Fine. He didn't just back off on his own."

"No kidding. So, what, Josh? What was it? You told him something embarrassing? Something stupid from when we were kids? Something I said in my sleep during a movie marathon you still tease me for?"

Josh opened his mouth, but I barreled on.

"Or did you just make it clear I was off-limits? Because that's what it felt like."

He didn't deny it.

And that was somehow worse than anything else he could've said.

"I just ..." His voice finally broke through. "I didn't mean to make you feel alone."

"Not physically," I said softly. My throat felt tight. "But, yeah, that's exactly how I felt."

I looked down at my feet, then back up at him. "You know what? It's fine."

"Brielle."

"I'm done pushing on this. It's not worth it. It's late. I'm tired. I'm just gonna go to bed."

He took a step forward. "Don't you want to watch another episode of our show?"

"No," I said. "Not tonight."

"Please? I ... I want to know what happens next. And tomorrow's going to be long. Faculty meeting. No one ever brings fresh doughnuts or the good flavors. It's all Boston cream or jelly-filled."

He was trying to be funny, but I really didn't want to laugh or smile at him. Not right now.

I folded my arms. "You can go ahead. I'll catch up on it later."

His face fell. That was the first crack.

"You sure?"

"Yeah. Maybe if I have time tomorrow I'll just watch it by myself."

I could already feel the maybe turning into a no. For the last few weeks, any excuse to spend more time with Josh had felt like a gift. But now? Now I didn't want to sit beside him and pretend we were fine when we weren't.

He looked down, shoved his hands into his pockets.

"Wait. One episode?" he asked quietly. "You don't even have to sit by me. I'd rather not watch it alone. Please, Brielle?"

God, he knew me too well. He knew I hated being behind. He knew I wouldn't be able to resist.

I sighed. "Fine. One episode."

He nodded, and it looked like relief swept through his shoulders. "Thank you."

I grabbed a throw blanket and sat on the opposite end of the couch.

And when the episode started, I didn't lean into him. I

didn't nudge his foot with mine. I didn't laugh when he muttered a commentary under his breath.

I just watched the screen. Focused hard. Waited for the credits.

Because I needed the reminder.

There was nothing between us.

There was never anything between us.

No matter how much I wished otherwise.

"You're still mad at me."

"Josh," I sighed. "Just drop it. Let's watch the show, or I will walk away. Don't ... don't ruin this."

That seemed to shut him up—for all of two minutes.

"Fine. You want to know what happened?" Before I could give him an answer, he powered on. "Matt didn't back off because of you. Nothing about you was the issue, and I hadn't exposed some embarrassing childhood truth about you to him. It's not that he has anything against you. He just, uh, didn't realize until he came into the kitchen that I ... that I cared about you so much."

Wait. What?

"Care about me?"

I forced myself not to ask him, *Like a friend, right?*

I didn't have to as I turned to face him on the couch. Those little moments up to now all started to piece together like a puzzle. His extra-long look at me that I'd pushed off as him seeing something on my face or just being polite when I was talking. The moments when I had thought that maybe he liked me just as much as I liked him.

Though neither of us said anything.

Not now.

"Not just like a friend," he said, as if reading my mind. He rubbed the back of his head. "Not just like my sister's friend either. I'm pretty sure it's obvious. I'm pretty sure that we are both obvious."

Heat flared to my cheeks. "O-oh."

"Oh ..." He paused before a chuckle burst out of him, eyes wide. He swallowed shakily. "That's what you are going to say after you pried it out of me?"

"I, um ... I don't know what you want me to say."

"I don't think I do either."

We both sat there on the couch in silence as the television screen lit up between us. I kept my gaze forward, locked on it, so I wouldn't look at him again in the silence. If I did, I wasn't sure what would happen or even what I wanted to happen. I could jump him. He could jump me. I could say something that I would regret. Likely that.

Most likely that.

But I thought I had it under control now, until my fat mouth and I couldn't stand it anymore. "You—you know how I felt about you."

Josh's head snapped toward me. "*Felt*."

"Yes."

"*Felt*. Like before? Like you used to feel something for me, Brielle?"

"Yes." My voice was tight. Controlled.

And I looked at him. Really looked at him. Into those eyes that suddenly felt like they were pulling me into something I couldn't climb out of, even if I wanted to.

"*Felt*, Josh. I felt so much for you. The last time I saw you, in your laundry room, I told you. I showed you. I've always felt everything when it came to you. And, sure, maybe I covered it up or pretended not to care. But even when I hated you, I still ..." I swallowed hard. "I still cared. Not like a friend. Definitely not like I should've."

Josh's expression didn't move. Except in his eyes—those

were flicking back and forth, like he was trying to decide if he was allowed to breathe yet.

"So ... felt back then," he repeated. "Not now."

"Felt ... always. Felt then." My voice cracked, and I hated that it did. "Felt after. Felt a week ago. Felt a second ago."

His hand shifted closer to me on the couch. He was leaning in. The heat of his body, the way his eyes dropped briefly to my lips—

"Feel now," I whispered.

Josh didn't say anything at first. His face was unreadable for half a breath. Then his jaw tensed, then softened. "I didn't realize either," he said, quieter. "But ... I've kind of been feeling something too. More than something. I just didn't know how to —how to deal with it."

"We can't *deal* with it."

"Maybe not."

"There's no maybe about it," I cut in. "You know how Gina would react."

"Do we?"

"Josh." I gave him a look. "And I'm not going to wreck this."

"This?"

"All of this," I said, gesturing between us. The apartment. Everything we'd rebuilt since he moved in. "I don't want to ruin it."

He hesitated. "How would Gina react?"

"She would ..." My throat tightened. I didn't want to say it out loud. Didn't want to break the fragile truth hanging between us. "She would think this is a betrayal," I finally said. "She once ditched a friend sophomore year just because she'd admitted she thought you were cute. And, yeah, that was high school. But this? This would be worse."

Josh nodded slowly. But his eyes never left mine.

His voice was lower. Honest. "I like you, Brielle."

"No, you don't."

"Yes, I do. More than like."

I shook my head. "No, you can't. Because then ..."

"Then?"

"Then I'd have to wonder why you treated me like crap for years," I said, the words spilling faster than I could stop them. "I'd have to make sense of that version of you. The one who made me feel so small. Like I was ridiculous for ever thinking I was enough to even matter to you. I'd have to believe I was just some stupid girl who couldn't even make it past a second date with twelve different guys in a month."

Josh blinked. "Nine. Technically eight."

"You're correcting me right now?"

He sighed. "That year you came home from college ..." His voice quieted. "I was a jerk. And I've told you that. But I didn't say I was sorry. Not really. And I am. I'm so sorry for how I treated you, Brielle. I toyed with you, and I teased you because I didn't know how to deal with how I felt. You were braver than I ever was. You showed up for your feelings. I hid from mine."

My heart thudded painfully in my chest.

Josh gave a slow, almost-shy smile. "I think I've had a crush on you for a long time. Stupid, right? Like we're back in school again."

"It's not stupid," I said, barely above a whisper. "But ..."

I looked at him. He was so close. Too close. And every part of me wanted to lean in, to say yes, to crash into this like it was something safe instead of terrifying.

But it was terrifying.

God, I wondered how his lips would feel against mine.

It would be all too simple.

It would be all too wonderful.

There was no hesitation between us. The only thing that was rolling through my entire body was lust for him that had never been sated from the moment I'd first known I loved my best friend's brother.

There was also fear.

What if he shoved me away again, just like he had all those years ago? What if he laughed in my face, just like he had before? He could.

This could all be a lie.

All the feeling and emotion was rising up inside me. I was a bundle of fear and hope and excitement. I wasn't sure what I should be feeling, and my body was already deciding for me.

"Are you crying?"

I shook my head, though his thumbs were already wiping away silent tears. "I'm not."

"There's evidence to the contrary." He chuckled, and then his smile turned downward. "What did I do now?"

"Nothing."

"I must've done something."

"No," I insisted. "You haven't. You haven't. I just keep waiting ..."

His hand drifted from the side of my neck to my shoulder and down until he grasped my hand.

I stared down at it, feeling numb and also like I had been electrocuted, unable to move.

"For what?"

I snapped my attention back to his face. "For you to laugh at me."

"What?"

"For you to say, *Just kidding*, like you did when I was in high school. Or maybe that this will last until the morning, and then you'll say that it was a mistake."

He was already shaking his head. "No, no, no, Bri. Nothing between us will ever be a mistake."

"But it has been."

"I was the mistake. Never you. I'm so sorry I ever made you feel that way."

"Will you again?" I asked.

He didn't answer right away.

"He's not ready to date someone like you," he'd said about his friend.

But what about him?

Did he deserve me?

Did he think that he did?

"No," he said. "I won't. I promise."

Something inside of me needed to hear those words. "You sure?"

"I want to be. Yes, I am."

"How can you be positive now?"

"Because I'm not the same person I was before. You know that. Since I was in that accident, I have been running around, trying to live as much life as I possibly could, and yet everywhere I went, it was the oddest thing. I went to Thailand. I went to Italy. I went to just about anywhere I could afford to, and when I ended up at one of the historical buildings or saw a person eating gelato on the side of the street, I thought of you. I thought of you all the time and the stories you'd probably be telling me as we traveled together."

"It's been years."

"So?" he insisted. "Doesn't mean I fucked up any less. Doesn't mean that I haven't had plenty of time to recognize that I have been looking for our story in every experience and every relationship I tried to create on my own, but it doesn't work that way. It doesn't mean that when I looked at you then or now that I don't want to imagine what you taste like."

I didn't think it was possible, but I hissed.

I wanted him to find out.

I stared at him.

I needed him too. Maybe too much. Maybe more than I should, but he was sitting right in front of me, and ... maybe I needed a bit of life in me too.

Maybe I needed a little bit of him.

Maybe all of him, if he would actually give it.

"Maybe we just need to get this out of our systems. Maybe that is all this is. Then we can move on."

He nodded, still staring at me, as if he couldn't pry his eyes away. "Yeah, that could be it. But Brielle..."

"What?" I asked, waiting for him to finish what he was about to say.

He just smiled, shook his head. "Nothing."

I kissed him like I meant it. He kissed me like he did too.

twenty-one

HE PULLED me onto his lap in one smooth motion, and I followed his lead. Like a dance. Already, I could tell we'd be great partners.

I spread my legs over his thighs. I held the sides of his face, feeling the slight prickle of stubble along his jawline as I tilted his chin and turned his head up to meet me. Kiss after kiss, his tongue swept in to completely whisk me away to an entirely different world.

I didn't feel like I was sitting on an old couch in the middle of a living room turned bedroom, where the honks of cars and the buzz of the television behind us were our constant companion.

I was only with Josh.

I could only see Josh through each peek I took through my eyelashes to watch him kiss me.

I would only smell Josh and his earthy musk and sweet eucalyptus body wash.

I could only hear the small sounds that Josh made—from tiny, humming moans to the hitch of his breath when I swooped in for an even deeper kiss, deeper touch.

All I could feel was Josh.

I fell into the feeling of his hands and, dear Lord, his mouth. Each kiss deepened, and our bodies pressed together. Every touch, every caress sent shivers through me, igniting a heat that I had long ago tamped down when I believed once and for all that Josh would never like me and that my crush as a teenager —and even after that—was just a crush.

But this? This proved that theory wrong. It blew it completely out of the water.

I gasped against his mouth.

Josh's hands roamed my body with a hunger that matched my own, his touch setting my skin ablaze with need. My teeth grazed over his bottom lip, and he groaned.

I pulled away slightly, breathless and flushed, my eyes locking with his in a silent exchange of raw desire. Without a word, we both knew what was about to happen between us. It was inevitable, unstoppable.

His hands slid up over my arms to my shoulders, brushing the collar of my cardigan aside. He kissed over my collarbone until I reached up to help him the rest of the way, unbuttoning the top.

He chuckled. "Buttons."

I giggled with him as if it were some kind of joke we were both in on as he worked on the second one. "Buttons."

He placed a kiss wherever his fingertips grazed my bare skin. My chest was exposed where my cami lay, though the touch of lace pressed against the swell of my breasts.

"More layers," he growled. I arched into his touch, breath hitching to hold me back from begging for more. I ran my hands down his chest, pulling his shirt out from where it had gotten caught in his belt.

His abs twitched against my hands. "God."

"Sorry," I whispered into his neck. He nipped at mine. "My hands are cold."

"Don't you dare apologize. Ever."

Ever. Like we'd be doing this again. Like I still had everywhere to explore.

Every touch, every kiss, every whispered word felt like a new discovery. It was as if we were unraveling the mystery that had been waiting to be solved for years.

Our hands roamed and our bodies pressed closer together until it was just the two of us. I wanted more. More.

I could feel his heartbeat against my chest, matching the rapid pace of my own.

Pressing me back against the cushions, Josh lay over me, blocking everything out from my view and mind.

What else was there other than what was happening here right now?

Finding a job? So unimportant right now.

Twelve terrible dates? The bane of my singular existence, as well as whoever else had been drawn into the ridiculousness of it all.

Josh? Josh. Josh. *Josh.*

I laughed at my own train of thought. At me.

"What's so funny?"

I shook my head. "Everything."

That this is happening!

When he adjusted himself against me, I felt just how hard he was against my hip, and I sucked in another breath.

"Hopefully not everything," he whispered, trailing another press of his lips up toward my ear.

Definitely not. I pulled him back down to my mouth, needing all of him I could get. I should always be wrapped up in his arms, lost in his touch, falling for him more with every sped-up heartbeat.

I gasped—and not out of pleasure. I pulled my face away from Josh, although my hands were still fisted in his shirt, which was making its way up toward his head. I whipped toward a different sound. The sound of keys and a, "Shit," as they hit the hallway floor.

My eyes widened at Josh before he even seemed to understand the situation. But I caught on fast.

I shoved him back away from me until we were both sitting up on the couch. I quickly reached for my cardigan, managing one button before the heavy metal lock on the door turned.

Josh sat there, a little dumbstruck. Still looking at me.

Gina walked in. "Hellooo."

I scrambled back off another inch from Josh, even as his fingers pressed into my thigh, begging me for just one more second, which I wanted to give. My entire body ached to give all of myself to him.

But I couldn't as I watched Gina smile at the two of us.

"You're up late." Her brow furrowed. "Fall asleep? Your hair is crazy."

I reached up to touch one of my frizzy waves. "Oh, yeah. I must look like a mess."

Josh remained silent.

She chuckled. "You will not believe the day I had. Do you care if I complain? Or maybe it will be more of a rant? Either way, I have other people's drama to share, if you're interested in some vicarious tea."

I cleared my throat. "Absolutely."

"Fantastic." She grinned, heading into her bedroom. "Let me change. Be right back!"

Josh and I sat there in silence, the weight of what had almost happened hanging heavily in the air between us. I could feel his gaze burning into me. My heart was still racing from our close encounter, and I struggled to compose myself as Gina disappeared into her room.

As soon as the door clicked shut behind her, Josh turned to me with a look of urgency in his eyes.

Was he going to say the words I wanted my brain to scream even though it very much ... didn't?

That this was a mistake.

Though, it wasn't. Out of everything in my life, I could confidently say that our kiss didn't feel that way.

He adjusted, maybe to get up and make his way to the bathroom or leave altogether.

Maybe I should leave?

I made the move to stand, but his hand caught my wrist, gently pulling me back down to sit next to him.

A rasp of his voice whispered in my ear, "I don't think you're just something I can get out of my system, Brielle."

Worse, I didn't think he was something I could just get out of my system either.

That was certain now.

One hundred percent. And maybe ... maybe that was worse than anything else we could've done right now.

THE
DATES TILL CHRISTMAS

BY BRIELLE THOMPSON

DATE SEVEN

Location: Board game café.
First Impression: Showed up wearing a vest with a cartoon cat saying Don't Purr-sue Me.

Listen, I want to be kind. But this one … was a challenge. I'd barely had my latte when Date Seven began telling me about his "creative sabbatical," which mostly sounded like watching conspiracy videos and baking banana bread without the bananas. He didn't like bananas, or most fruit in general. The highlight came when he told me he still lived with his mom.

Which—fine!—people live with parents for all kinds of reasons. Housing is expensive. If anyone knows that right now, it's me. Life is complicated.

But then, he asked if I could walk him to the corner.

Why? Because his mom was picking him up. He didn't like adding to pollution, so he just never really saw the point of getting his driver's license. But he was also admittedly frightened of most forms of public transportation after he saw a rat scurrying down the tracks of the metro.

His mom pulled up in a nice, sleek SUV … with stickers on the back window. Of his face. And they were recent photographs.

Blind Date Status: Survived the café. Survived emotionally. May be seen on a bumper sticker near you.

Note to self (and all of you): It's hard to trust a man who calls you "m'lady" un-ironically before learning your name or looks like he may still flip the Monopoly board on a casual Thursday night.

twenty-two

JOSH and I tiptoed around the apartment, talking to each other in only pleasantries, for if we did any more, one of us would suddenly be on the edge of tearing the other's clothes off.

Now I was thinking about tearing his clothes off.

No. I needed to get back on track.

Getting on track with my life included continuing my schedule of two more dates, which had felt like I was being locked in a torture chamber. It wasn't that they weren't nice, though they each had their quirks. They were just...not Josh.

I took a deep breath as I smoothed out the black sweater dress I'd put on for Gina's first big art show opening. Since her work friends would already be there, answering questions and making sure everything ran smoothly, she had given Josh and me her two complimentary tickets.

"I just can't believe that none of your dates were winners," she said as she got ready for the big night. She lined her lips and applied a light sheen of lip gloss. "Or at least went into a second date."

I glanced at her. "You've heard how they went."

"I know …" She hesitated. "Are you sure you've been giving them a good chance? You're not just humoring me?"

I sighed. "Yes, Gina."

"Don't give me that. I'm being serious, but I also just want you to be happy. I appreciate that you're getting out there, and honestly, that was the main point for the dates."

"What do you mean?"

"Would it be freaking amazing for you to fall in love and have this great story? Of course. But it's also good to see you getting out of the house and kind of getting your spark back."

"My spark?"

"Yeah. I mean, not that you lost it. Just—you know what? I don't know what I'm saying. I feel like when we moved back in together, you were kind of serious and quiet and—you were stressed, I know. But lately, you've looked happier. Lighter. Maybe it's that you are writing again too. Writing actual fun stuff."

Or a few other things.

"You might be right." If anything, I did feel a bit less … stressed, like I had been before. Especially now that no new jobs were being posted anywhere for the rest of the year, it looked like.

"I really like that dress on you."

I glanced down at the simple dress. "Thank you."

"I'm sorry if I said something wrong."

"You didn't."

"I'm just so excited to have my friend here and now I'll finally have less work all the time so that we can celebrate the end of the year together. You're the best, and you always cheer me on." She wrapped her arms around my shoulders in the mirror. "Love you, Bri."

I smiled faintly, grateful for Gina's attempt to lift my spirits. "Love you too, Gi."

* * *

The art show was already in full swing by the time we arrived. The gallery buzzed with conversation and the soft clinking of glasses—which were filled with slightly better than decent sparkling wine—echoing off the stark white walls. Light reflected off gilded frames and glossy canvas textures, creating a warm glow across the sea of people in curated coats and careful shoes.

Almost immediately, Gina was swept into a tide of colleagues and admirers, disappearing with a beaming laugh and a glass already half empty. That left Josh and me standing by the entrance, hands awkwardly stuffed into pockets until the tray of wine got to us, each of us taking one.

I held my glass in both hands as his eyes settled on me, like a weight. A silent question. A thread pulled taut and fraying between us.

"I meant to make time before this to talk to you."

"Oh?"

"I'm sorry," Josh said quietly. His voice barely cut through the ambient hum of the room, but it still landed square in my chest. "I never meant for things to get this complicated between us."

"You didn't make anything get complicated," I said quickly —too quickly. "I mean ..."

"We need to talk. I can't just let this hang like it doesn't matter." His hands shifted deeper into the pockets of his dress pants, his jaw tightening. "I can't stand you ignoring me now. I didn't upset you, did I?"

"No," I said, the word catching in my throat. "Of course not."

"Because if I did—"

"You didn't."

His mouth pressed into a thin line. He didn't believe me.

Before I could say anything more, Gina reappeared, her energy like a gust of wind as she slipped between us, entirely oblivious to the storm we were standing in.

"Hey there!" she chirped, eyes bright as she scanned our faces. "How are you two enjoying it?"

"It's amazing, Gina," I said, forcing a smile as I glanced around the gallery. "It's crazy to think you helped put all this together."

She grinned, satisfied. "Right? And to think people said an art history degree was basically useless."

Josh huffed a short laugh and shook his head. "It's really impressive, Gina. Thanks for inviting us."

"Well," she said with a teasing scrunch of her nose, "I really just wanted Bri to come, but I didn't want to be rude by leaving you out."

"Appreciate that," Josh muttered, barely masking the edge in his voice.

But Gina was already turning back to me. "Come on. I have someone I want you to meet."

She grabbed my wrist and tugged me through the sea of guests. I stumbled for a moment, glancing over my shoulder just in time to catch Josh tipping back the rest of his drink, watching us with unreadable eyes.

We weaved past art collectors and press badges, between stretched canvases and minimalist sculptures. My nerves buzzed. Every step away from Josh made my thoughts louder, less manageable. When we finally stopped, Gina tugged me to a halt in front of a tall, clean-cut man in a navy blazer, who was sipping from a stemless glass of red.

"Brielle, this is Alex. He helped support the show and apparently has a thing for books. So, obviously, I thought of you."

"Alex," I repeated dumbly, blinking as he offered his hand.

He smiled warmly, showing off straight teeth and a hint of a dimple. "It's great to meet you. Gina's told me a lot about you."

I shot her a sideways glance. "A lot?"

She held up a hand. "An appropriate amount. Nothing that'll ruin your mystique."

Alex chuckled, his grip firm and easy. "She undersold it, honestly."

We fell into casual conversation about the show and books we'd both read. He asked about my writing, my newsletter, the kind of things I liked to explore in my work. It was easy. Comfortable even.

I knew Gina was watching from somewhere with smug satisfaction, probably thinking she was doing me a favor.

But I couldn't help glancing over my shoulder.

Josh stood across the gallery, half-heartedly chatting with one of Gina's friends. He was angled just enough to keep me in view.

He was watching.

I hated how much I noticed that.

Alex walked me over to another piece. In front of us hung an oil painting in heavy color blocks that didn't seem to have a focal point. I found myself nodding to whatever he was saying while counting the seconds until Josh moved again. And he did. Around another corner, like a ghost trailing just a little too close.

"You okay?" Alex asked gently.

"Oh, yeah. Sorry," I said, faking a laugh. "Just trying to take everything in."

"It's a lot. And honestly? I'm impressed by anyone who can navigate this kind of thing without wanting to hide in the corner."

I smiled at that. "Believe me, I've thought about it."

We chatted a bit more, his questions thoughtful and his laughter easy, but I couldn't shake the feeling crawling up my spine or the sight of Josh following us around the gallery.

Then came his voice behind me, low and firm.

"Sorry, need to steal her."

I turned, unsurprised. "Josh."

Alex blinked, his eyebrows lifting a little. "No problem. I'll catch up with you later?"

"Sure," I said a little too quickly.

Josh barely waited for Alex to turn away before speaking. "I couldn't watch that anymore."

I arched a brow. "Watch *what* exactly?"

His jaw clenched, but he didn't answer.

Neither did I. Not yet.

We stood there, in the middle of other people's art and other people's conversations, still stuck in the silence between whatever we were and whatever we weren't ready to be.

"He wasn't that bad. He was thoughtful and has passion for what he does," I said. "I get that."

"Sounds exciting."

I huffed, looking around for Gina, though she, too, was nowhere to be found. Right now, as Josh held me to his side, I wasn't sure if that was a good or bad thing.

Good, because it felt so *so* good.

Bad, well, because of everything else.

I thought maybe by the time we reached the far end of the gallery, he'd stop leading me, but he didn't. We kept drifting— his hand at my elbow, then not—until we ended up at a narrow hallway near the catering station. Servers moved in and out with trays of empty flutes and shrimp skewers, casting us quick, curious glances as they passed. One waitress raised her eyebrows at us before turning on her heel, no doubt eager to whisper to someone about the almost couple lingering by the storage door.

Even though we weren't a couple.

I closed my eyes for a moment and reminded myself of that.

"What are you doing?" I asked quietly.

"Talking."

I glanced around again. "Here?"

"It's the only place you won't pretend I'm not standing next to you."

That wasn't fair, but it wasn't wrong either.

"Okay," I said, breath hitching. "Talk."

"You haven't been talking to me."

"I'm talking to you now."

"You know what I mean, Bri."

I sighed.

"Fine. Then just tell me why we can't ..."

"Can't what?"

"Be together," Josh said. "I kept waiting for you to talk with me again after the other night and then you just ignored me completely again."

"That's not what I was trying to do," I said.

"Wasn't it?"

"No. Not exactly."

Josh blinked, but his voice didn't hesitate. "I don't think I need to remind you just how much I like you and want to be with you now, but I can. Do you want me to?"

I wanted him to say it again and again until it rewrote all the memories of him walking away. "I'm scared."

His chest bowed as he let out a deep breath, a small smile on his lips. "That's ok. So am I, but I'm told in life that's what makes it's worthwhile, isn't it?"

Coming from the guy that just last year was traveling the world and skydiving.

"What if ..."

"What if what?" he asked, though we both already knew. "What if Gina finds out? Honestly, I feel like my sister couldn't be more oblivious to anything that isn't about her right now. I think we're safe."

I folded my arms, glaring. "Don't be a jerk. I was her friend first."

"I know," he said, softer this time. "I'm sorry. I just ... I've been trying to talk to you for days. You've been avoiding me."

"Because it's the only thing I can think to do. So this can all just ... pass."

"I told you," he said, stepping closer, "you're not something I want to get out of my system, Brielle."

"We could still—"

"Try?" he interrupted. "No. Even that kiss was enough to tell me that if I ever get to kiss you again, I want everything. I want all of it. All of you."

The words made something in my chest crack open. Joy and fear and a deep ache tangled together, sparking like faulty wiring.

He reached out, tentative. "Just give me a chance. One that's on your terms. You can even kiss me and then tell me it was a mistake after. Say I'm terrible at it. That I misread everything. But let this be yours. Not mine. Not anyone else's."

My voice was barely above a whisper. "What are we even doing?"

"Are you really going to make me say it again?"

"My friendship with your sister ..."

"I know." He ran a hand through his hair. "But I don't care what she thinks."

"I do," I said, and I hated the tremble in my voice. "I care. A lot."

Josh studied me like he was trying to memorize something.

Like maybe if he stared long enough, I'd say something different.

"Then you've made your decision?" he asked quietly.

"I think ... I think I have to."

He sucked on the inside of his cheek, trying not to react.

"Are you doing this to get back at me?" he asked. "For what happened at Christmas. That night."

"I thought you said you didn't remember."

"Of course I remember. You told me how you felt, and I shut you down like a goddamn idiot. I was scared then. I was a coward. But I'm not anymore. I'm here. I'm trying."

His voice cracked a little, and that somehow made it worse.

"I'm willing to be brave now, Brielle. But I need you to be brave with me. Because we can't control how anyone else reacts —not Gina, not anyone. We only get to choose us."

But I wasn't so sure I could.

I didn't have a job. I barely had a social circle in this city. And now Josh was asking me to risk the one stable thing that had remained through all of it—his family, Gina, the holidays, the safety of the role I played in their lives.

I couldn't shake the voice in the back of my head. The one that asked, *What happens when he leaves again? What happens when he decides he can't stay?*

Because people always seemed to leave.

My jaw trembled. I tried to answer, but couldn't find the words.

Josh waited. And when I didn't speak, he slowly nodded.

"All right," he whispered.

"Josh ..."

He paused.

"I can't lose her," I said finally. "You don't get it. You and Gina and your family are the only constant I've had."

"I'll still be here," he said. "But ..."

He didn't finish. He didn't need to.

I looked down at my nails, red polish already chipped at the edges, and focused on breathing. Anything to stop the tears from coming.

But when I lifted my head, Josh was gone.

Quiet tears tracked down my cheeks anyway.

THE 12 DATES TILL CHRISTMAS

BY BRIELLE THOMPSON

DATE TEN

Location: Used bookstore turned coffee shop.
First Impression: Spoiler: He was wonderful. Almost.

We bonded over books, talked about the strange rhythm of growing up and growing apart from who you used to be. He told me about his failed first novel. I told him about my past college internship that paid in tote bags and granola bars. When he smiled, I felt it in my chest. Not butterflies. More like … grounding. The opposite of my recently dating fight or flight responses.

It was like someone was reminding me that maybe it wasn't too late to be hopeful.

But—of course there's a but—he's moving to Chicago in January. And he told me that up front. No games. No see where it goes. Just honesty. He also just got out of a long term relationship and wasn't quite sure if he was ready to move on yet.

So, maybe this wasn't the one.

Maybe I just really wanted him to be.

Blind Date Status: Restored faith in dating. Bought a book I didn't need. The holidays as approaching and I think maybe I should've called this newsletter series "The Ten Dates Till Christmas."

Because I'm ready for the end of this adventure.

twenty-three

I COULDN'T STOP THINKING about Josh. I had to stop.

I needed to stop. It was over. Done.

It was easier that way.

Though, every time I blinked too long or let my mind wander for more than a second, there he was again. His crooked half smile, the way his laugh curled at the end of a sentence, that one perfect second when his hand had cupped the side of my face like I was something precious.

It was all still there.

Worse, it wasn't even the kiss that haunted me most. It was everything around it. The way we fit. Like the smallest puzzle pieces that only ever had one right place to go.

And now it was just ... silence.

Unsaid and unresolved and unbearable.

I shoved a few last-minute things into my overnight bag and unzipped the front pocket to double-check if I had enough underwear packed. Not exactly the romantic start to a holiday homecoming, but if I forgot something, Gina would never let me live it down. She was already threatening to leave me behind.

The drive home was slow. Slower than usual, like the car was dragging its feet too.

Josh drove. Gina rode shotgun. She insisted on playing her holiday playlist, which was mostly glittery remixes of nostalgic songs in no particular order. The sound filled every inch of the car. The music was loud enough to make talking impossible, which I approved of for once.

Josh barely spoke. Except when he commented on the playlist with a dry, "This one? Really?" or, "Wasn't this track just playing?"

I sat behind him in the back seat, my head resting against the cold window, breath fogging the glass slightly.

Outside, the city fell away slowly—lights thinning into suburbs, storefronts giving way to empty lots and stretches of dark, familiar roads. I let my eyes close, half dozing.

Sleep hadn't been kind to me lately. Not when every time I closed my eyes, I imagined Josh saying, "I want all of it. All of you," and I woke up, aching with the fact that I still wanted him too.

"Hey!" Gina's voice snapped me out it. "Do you want to drive by your old house?"

My eyes flew open. "What? No. I'm good. Thanks."

She made a vague sound, like she didn't quite understand, but wasn't going to argue. "All righty then."

The car grew quiet again, except for the distant crooning of some Christmas song I couldn't pay attention to. I shifted uncomfortably in my seat.

In the rearview mirror, Josh glanced at me. His eyes caught mine for just a second; it was brief, but something passed between us anyway. Maybe guilt. Maybe apology. Maybe nothing at all.

I looked away.

He took the next turn, bypassing the street I hadn't driven down in years. The one with the leaning mailbox and the uneven sidewalk slabs. The house with the chipped paint and the rusting fence. My house. Or at least, what used to be.

When I'd left the last time, I'd made a promise to myself that it would be the final time. That I wouldn't be one of those people who looked back. There wasn't anything left to return to anyway. The family was gone, the furniture was sold, and the memories ... well, the ones worth keeping had already been packed up and taken with me. The rest could rot under the weight of their own silence.

Josh didn't say anything else. Neither did I.

The tires crunched onto a more familiar driveway a few minutes later—his parents' house. It was warm light and tidy bricks and a wreath on the door, too big to be tasteful. The kind of place where nothing really changed, and yet everything felt different when you came back.

Gina jumped out first, excited to be home.

Josh paused. Turned off the ignition, but didn't move.

I opened my door, hand gripping the strap of my bag tightly. He still hadn't said a word to me directly.

"Josh."

He opened his door and stepped out. "Welcome home, Brielle."

Gina looked at me and then up toward Josh, who said his hellos inside quickly before making his way up the steps away from everyone.

Mrs. Hutton released me from a hug to look between us all. "Did something happen on the ride?"

"He's been like that lately," Gina said with an unconcerned shrug.

"Huh," she sighed. "Hopefully, he isn't unhappy. I thought that since he came back from his trip, he was enjoying his position at the school."

"He is," I interjected, trying to soothe her worries.

Both women turned to look at me.

"He is," I repeated. "Josh told me how much he enjoys his new job. The work is simple, but he's been making friends with people on the staff."

"Wow," Mrs. Hutton looked back towards the stairs again where he went. "Then I wonder what is going on with him."

"How did you know that?" asked Gina.

"Know what?"

"That he's been enjoying school and that fundraiser thing?" Gina clarified.

"Oh, well, we've just been talking more at home when you were at work, and I asked," I said. That wasn't a lie, though for some reason, my heart started to rocket in my chest a little faster, as if I needed to come up with one—and quick.

"You two should go up as well. unpack and get yourself settled," suggested Mrs. Hutton.

Gina nodded, making it up to steps before she turned back to her mom. "Do you need help with anything for the party tomorrow?"

She smiled. "I would love some help with baking actually if you two girls would like to join me."

* * *

The warmth of the Huttons' kitchen wrapped around me like a favorite blanket, comforting and almost painfully familiar. The scent of cinnamon, nutmeg, and browned butter filled the air, thick and sweet, clinging to my sweater sleeves as I tied one of

Mrs. Hutton's faded floral aprons around my waist. It smelled faintly of vanilla and peppermint, like it had absorbed a decade of holiday cookie making.

The granite countertop was a flurry of flour and sugar. Gingerbread dough had been cut into rows of stiff little men and stars, waiting for their turn in the oven.

My fingers moved without thinking, rolling and pressing cookie cutters into the soft dough, but my mind kept slipping back upstairs.

Josh's footsteps had become a phantom sound I couldn't stop hearing, even when they weren't there. Just like his laugh. Just like the memory of his lips on mine.

"So, you're sticking to the plan of all the usual cookies this year?" Gina asked, trying to make casual conversation since it didn't seem like I was going to start any, though that wasn't anything new here.

"You bet," agreed her mom. "Everyone always asks for the iced sugar cookies. You know that. It wouldn't be Christmas without them."

Gina, who was sifting flour into a bowl, flashed her usual easy grin as she reached toward the basket holding each small, laminated note card.

I smiled at the familiar sight, glancing at Mrs. Hutton again, in her own little world, much like Gina when she got in the zone. She hummed as she worked.

A sharp bang came from upstairs; someone—clearly Josh— had dropped something loud and heavy.

Mrs. Hutton looked up toward the ceiling with a long-suffering sigh. "That boy," she muttered, though her tone was affectionate.

I didn't look. Couldn't. I focused on slicing the legs off a slightly-too-thin gingerbread man, the edge of the cookie cutter wobbling in my grip.

"So, Brielle, any big plans?" Mrs. Hutton asked, her voice warm and inviting. "I can imagine that so much has happened for you this year since graduating. Gina has been so busy lately. I bet you're looking forward to a little time off as well."

I snapped out of my thoughts and looked up. My cheeks flushed. "Uh, yeah, definitely," I replied, trying to recover while Gina bit her bottom lip, looking guilty for not filling her mom in on just how unsimilar my and Gina's work life situation had been. "I mean, work has been ... busy. I've been accepting a lot of freelance writing projects. But I'm excited for some down-time before getting back to the job hunt, looking for something full-time in the new year."

Mrs. Hutton raised an eyebrow, clearly sensing my hesita-tion. "You still haven't found anything permanent, huh?"

I wasn't sure how much I wanted to admit about my frus-trations, especially in front of Gina's mom. I didn't want her to think that I was failing or that Gina might be struggling under the responsibility of keeping us and the apartment afloat. Because she wasn't. I was pulling my weight no matter what I needed to do to make it happen.

I gave a small shrug and forced a smile. "I'm still looking. But you know, keeping my options open." I cleared my throat, trying to let the subject die. "I'm sure something will come along soon enough."

Mrs. Hutton smiled again, this time softer, her eyes kind. "You always were a smart one. I'm sure the right thing is just around the corner."

Gina gave a tiny snort. "Or a rich husband."

I bumped her with my hip. "Thanks for the vote of confidence."

But the joke felt hollow. And no matter how hard I tried to focus on the gingerbread, the conversation, or even the familiar thrum of holiday anticipation in this house, Josh was still there. Literally, he was just above my head and impossible to ignore.

Gina's eyes lit up with mischief as she sensed the switch. "She's been on quite a few dates lately. My friends have been setting her up."

"Aw, that's so fun."

Some of the time.

Instead of saying that, I winced inwardly and plastered a smile on my face. "Well, uh, they've been ... nice. Nice guys, you know? Just not really ..."

Mrs. Hutton smiled, clearly amused. "Ah, got it. You never know. I hope that Gina might go on some dates and settle down before I'm too old to enjoy her wedding and grandbabies."

"Mom, I'm twenty-five."

"I married your father at twenty-four. It's not crazy."

"It's a different world," Gina replied dryly. "Chill out. Put those expectations on your older child."

She sighed. "I've given up on him. Josh always goes off and does what I least expect."

"Are you talking about me?"

Josh made his way down the steps, turning into the kitchen. None of us answered.

"Okay then. I'm headed out to meet up with some friends if anyone needs me."

"Brielle was just telling us about how you took her to that fundraiser of yours at school recently."

His eyebrows arched an inch high. "Oh, yeah. It was, uh, a really good time there, wrapping." He glanced at me.

"Speed-wrapping."

He chuckled. "Right. Surprised you want to admit to that when I beat you."

"You said it wasn't a competition."

He rolled his eyes with a smile.

Gina cleared her throat. "Sounds like the most fun thing I've ever heard," she said sarcastically.

I shrugged. "It was fun."

"Yeah, it was good, until her date bailed on her for the night, and we went to my friend Matt's house for holiday movies."

"You went to his friend's house with him?" Gina asked.

Had I not told her that before?

"I was already dressed to go out," I said softly.

Slowly, she nodded, studying me, as if this made some kind of sense.

I hoped my face wasn't as red as it felt.

His mom smiled. "Mmhmm. Well, have fun out. Let me know if you'll be back for dinner."

"Will do."

"Have fun," I added.

Josh paused, looking at me for another moment before giving a single nod. He half lifted his hand as he turned around. "See ya later."

Mrs. Hutton's eyes were on me.

I looked back to my gingerbread, transferring them over to the tray to go into the oven.

"Well, don't give up just yet, Brielle."

"What?" I asked, confused what we were talking about now. "Did I miss something?"

"Your dates," she said, reminding me of the conversation we had been having prior to Josh walking in. "Don't worry. The right one is out there."

"I'm just happy she isn't locking herself up in the apartment."

"Seems like she has been getting out quite a bit." Mrs. Hutton shot me a sly look. "Maybe the right one is closer than you think."

My eyes widened. I wasn't sure if Mrs. Hutton was hinting at something or if it was just my imagination running wild. I'd only just gotten here, and Josh had walked into the room for what, all of a minute, maybe two? No way.

"I'm just … focusing on finding a job right now," I said, my voice a little too high-pitched.

I rolled out another section of dough, willing myself not to think about Josh's warm smile or the way he had been looking at me lately. No one else had noticed, but I knew.

I let out a breath, heart still racing. My stress levels had been through the roof recently. I needed to get my head on straight. Focus on baking. Focus on work and writing. Focus on anything other than the fact that Josh was living in the same house, which felt even more intimate than the apartment for some reason, and the way he looked at me, like he was trying to tell me something without saying a word.

At least … until the holidays were over and I was out of this pressure cooker of it all.

Future me could deal with that.

I could curse now me later.

"I actually have one Christmas present for you early," said Gina, coming up next to me. "You good here, Mom?"

"Go," she said with a little less of a smile, though her voice remained upbeat. "Enjoy yourself."

I took the hand towel from her, wiping my hands.

"What are you talking about?" I asked Gina.

She'd better not have gotten me anything extra. I had already been stressed over what to get her this year, maxing out my present budget to make sure it was something worthwhile with how great she had been to me since we'd moved in together.

"You didn't need to get me anything, let alone something extra."

"Psh." Gina waved me off.

Mrs. Hutton smiled without saying anything. Her eyes flickered when they landed on me again, as if studying.

Gina took my hand tightly. "You just have to follow me."

"Could you slow down? I'm going to face-plant in your front yard again."

Gina glanced back at me with that mischievous grin that always meant trouble. "But this time, you're sober. So, maybe your pretty face will stand a chance."

I groaned, yanking my coat around my shoulders at the front door along with her before she half dragged me across the porch and down the icy front steps. "That was senior year, Gina. Are you ever going to let the incident go?"

"Not a chance. It's a classic."

The cold hit my cheeks in a sharp burst. It was the kind of winter air that turned breath into clouds and made my fingers ache, even through gloves. Gina was practically bouncing beside me, bundled in a puffy coat and a knit scarf that looked like it had been woven by a very enthusiastic grandmother.

"My personal blind date pick is here. At last!" she chirped, like this was the grand finale to a months-long game show.

I arched a brow. "I thought Alex from the gallery was your pick."

"Nope. He was a convenient wild card. Don't be mistaken." She twirled on her booted heels, gesturing out toward the driveway. "This my real pick."

I chuckled under my breath. "We're at home. Who could you possibly have—"

But I stopped.

Because I saw him.

And everything inside me stilled.

He was standing by the mailbox, hands shoved into the pockets of a sleek wool coat, hair styled just like it had always been—neatly tousled, like he never had to try. A familiar smirk twitched at the corners of his mouth the moment our eyes met, like no time had passed at all.

I felt the blood drain from my face. "Gina ... is that ..."

She grinned. "You're welcome."

My ex-boyfriend.

From high school.

twenty-four

WHY?

That was the first question that popped into my head and to be honest for a long moment, I couldn't move beyond that. Just... *Why?*

The boy I had fallen for when I was seventeen and heartbreak still felt romantic instead of exhausting was standing in front of me. The boy who had written a poem about my laugh in my yearbook and then dumped me two weeks before graduation because he was going off to find himself at college, was standing in front of me with his hands in his coat pockets, boots coated around the toe with a light sheen of slush.

I turned towards Gina who looked as if she might explode with delight.

"Why," I asked slowly, "would you do this to me?"

"You said you were open to being set up until Christmas, didn't you? And you need to stop living in your head, Bri. You've been moody since we left the city—"

"I have not been moody."

"You literally cried into a gingerbread cookie I'd picked up from the bodega yesterday."

I didn't have a very good answer to that. "It was a very emotional cookie."

Gina crossed her arms, unconvinced. "You need closure. Or a rebound. Or both. So, bam! Closure, wrapped in a cute scarf."

I turned back to look at Brenden. He was waving now.

And smiling.

That smile. Charming. Harmless. And now entirely unwelcome.

My heart beat faster, but not the way it used to. Not with fluttery nerves or first-date jitters. This was confusion, unease. Something restless in my chest.

My voice was quiet when I said, "I thought I was done with the blind dates, Gina."

"But you haven't found your holiday sweetheart," she said. "And don't lie to me, this one feels right, doesn't it? You're back here in town where everything started and so is he. You're both together again.

Both together again.

Josh flashed back to my mind.

"I can't do this."

"Sure you can." Gina nudged me forward. "Just say hi. One drink. Maybe a holiday miracle."

I turned to her, my breath fogging between us. "Did Josh know you were doing this?"

Gina shrugged. "Why would he care?"

But I cared.

I cared far too much.

* * *

My high school boyfriend, Brenden, stood on the edge of the sidewalk, letting me take my time. Behind him, I glanced at his car that was in just as good condition as when his parents had bought it for him for high-school graduation.

There was a soft look in his eyes. My heart still hammered in my chest, but at least, less so?

And also a whole lot more so.

My shoulders slumped. I mean, I knew Brenden. I'd been sick with Brenden and gone through awkward high school drama with him. It certainly wasn't like I was suddenly on another blind date. Not at all.

What was going on here?

"Hey, Brielle." The corner of Brenden's lip curled up into a half smile.

He looked just about as awkward as I felt right now.

I couldn't believe it. He was here. Right in front of me. This was Gina's pick? Brenden was my final date before Christmas? I guess...

Well, it could certainly be so much worse.

Before I knew it I was swept up in a long hug. "It's good to see you too Brenden."

"I'll just leave you two here to get along. Have fun!" Gina squealed as she headed back into the house.

Once I was released from the hug, I turned to watch Gina's retreating figure, feeling a mix of gratitude and frustration. Was this her wingwoman move? Because this was now the second time that she had stuck me in front of a guy and run away.

Why did she always have to meddle in my love life? And why had she thought Brenden was the right choice for me? I mean, he had been. Once.

I turned back to Brenden, who was still standing there with that same soft look in his eyes.

"So ... Brenden," I started, not sure where to begin. "What are you doing here?"

He shifted on his feet, seemingly nervous. "I heard you were back in town for the holidays, and I thought it might be nice to catch up. See how you've been."

I couldn't help but feel a pang of nostalgia at his words. Brenden and I had been close once, before life took us on different paths. But here he was, holding a red flower and looking at me like maybe there was still something between us.

As we stood there in the fading light of the quickly turning winter evening in front of a house from my childhood, I realized that maybe Gina's matchmaking wasn't so terrible after all. Perhaps this unexpected reunion with Brenden was exactly what I needed to face the unresolved feelings from our past and finally find closure.

Maybe it would help me get over Josh. Or at least forget about him for a few hours.

Josh, Josh, Josh.

Bah!

"Ready for our blind date?" He chuckled.

I couldn't help but laugh with him. "Yes. Let's do this."

What was happening with my life?

twenty-five

HOLIDAY LIGHTS TWINKLED along Main Street, their soft glow reflecting off the crisp snow that had started to fall.

I tucked my hands into my coat pockets, my breath puffing out in little clouds in front of me as I walked beside Brenden, my childhood best friend turned high-school boyfriend turned ... well, not quite a stranger, but something in that general vicinity.

It had been years since we'd seen each other. We were no longer teenagers, but still with a history between us, and that history was heavy with memories of first love and first heartbreaks.

Or something like that.

Brenden, always the easygoing type, cracked jokes like he used to. His deep laugh was infectious in the quiet winter night as we walked.

I smiled, glancing at him from the corner of my eye.

"I swear, this town has never changed," I said, keeping my voice light. Though there was still hesitancy as I looked around as we walked.

The town was just about the same as I remembered it, and it wasn't as if I'd never visited home with Gina when we were on school breaks, but now it felt different. I felt different.

"I mean, look at this. Snow is falling on the same slightly run-down shops."

Brenden grinned. "It's strange to think, but I think I missed this place a little."

"You haven't been back recently?"

He shook his head as his hand reached down and brushed against mine. "Busy. But this year I promised my mom that I'd be home for the holidays."

"That's nice of you to find the time," I said.

"Come on," he said. "This is your first time back here in a while, isn't it?"

I shrugged, looking down at our feet and back up to Brenden's face. He sniffed, jostling the bridge of his glasses that tipped slightly to the side. It was as if I was back in high school walking outside when we had no money and nowhere really to go.

It was easy to fall into our old rhythm. Almost carefree.

Or maybe, lately, I had just gotten too used to struggling all the time.

"I'm probably going to be around more often though for my mom, so don't go feeling bad for her," said Brenden. "I'm actually planning to move into the city soon."

I whipped to look at him. "You are?"

"Yeah, I got a job offer. Seemed like a good option. When I get there you'll have to show me all the cool places around." He nudged me playfully with his shoulder.

It was impossible not to feel the chemistry. Maybe the young, vibrant attraction we had between us in high school could never go away. Did that kind of thing just disappear?

Even buried under all the years of other friends and relation-ships and distance?

There were moments—when our hands brushed, when our familiar gazes lingered for just a second too long—that made me question whether I could just slip back into the past and pick up where we'd left off, probably just like Gina had thought.

But could I? Could we?

Did I want to?

I caught Brenden glancing at me as we passed the old school bell tower on the edge of town. His eyes softened as he took a deep breath.

"Do you ever miss it?" he asked, his voice quieter now. "Us, I mean. Back when things were simpler?"

Another pang of nostalgia hit me in the chest, sharp and sudden.

"I wouldn't call high school simpler. But sometimes," I admitted, stopping in my tracks and looking up at the tower. "But I don't know if I miss us or if I miss who we were then."

Brenden's brow furrowed slightly, and he turned to face me, hands jammed into the pockets of his coat. "I get that. I think I've changed a lot since then."

"You think?" I raised an eyebrow at him.

"Okay, I've definitely changed. I'm not the same guy you dated in high school, Bri. But ..." He paused, as if trying to find the right words. "But that doesn't mean the old parts of me are completely gone. The ones you liked, I mean. The ones you ..." His voice trailed off, leaving the space between us heavier than before.

Tightness coiled in my chest. I was glad I still had my hot chocolate cup to hold in my hands as my thumb scraped against the side of the plastic lid.

"Just like I'm sure you've changed too. For the better. We're adults now." He smiled. "Though I can see that you're still the cute, funny, smart, creative girl I knew. At least from what Gina was telling me. It surprised me when she reached out, but I couldn't help but feel like it was right, you know?"

"I know," I whispered. "I just ... I'm not sure I'm the same person I was either in a lot of ways even though it may seem like it."

"I get that. Trust me, I get that."

"Maybe that's what makes this feel so strange. I'm sure Gina had good intentions."

Brenden reached out and tucked on my hand to stop. He stepped a little closer, his eyes locking on to mine with an intensity that made my heart race.

"Maybe," he said softly. "But maybe that's not such a bad thing. Maybe it means we can learn about who we are now and if we still fit. I mean, I think we do, more or less. It feels like we would."

I took a deep breath.

This was sort of what I had hoped would happen, wasn't it? That someone would fall into my life? Sure, I hadn't expected it to be someone I already knew, but ...

I looked at Brenden and smiled.

Could we really figure this out after so long? We *were* kids. Or breakup was natural in a way when we were going in different directions. I didn't have hard feelings towards Brenden. I wouldn't be walking out in the cold with him if I did.

I shook my head slightly, the cold air biting at my cheeks. "I don't know, Brenden. I don't want to mess things up. This is nice."

"I agree."

"Really nice to see you, honestly. But ..."

He smiled gently, his thumb brushing against my cold knuckles. "We don't have to decide anything out tonight. This is a carefree, casual date! We'll take it one step at a time."

There was another part of Brenden I had known from high school.

He always had a plan. He was so straightforward and logical at all times.

It was easy to let him take the lead.

"Because I'd really like to see you again. Sounds cheesy, but it's really been too long. I know you're not ready to jump back into anything. At least, that's the vibe I'm getting, aside from, ya know, the dozen dates you've been on lately."

I covered my face with my hands.

He laughed again, not deterred. "But I keep thinking that this feels a little too good to be true—that Gina reached out to me and we are both single at the same time. I'd like to see where this goes. If you're willing."

I hesitated, the weight of the decision pressing down. I wasn't sure, couldn't be sure, but the thought of walking away now felt just as wrong as letting things slip back to the way they used to be.

"I'm willing," I answered at last, drawing out each word. My voice was somehow steady despite the flurry of emotions constantly coursing through my body. "I'm just not sure where it'll lead."

Brenden reached out, his fingers brushing mine again. "Neither am I. But I think it'll be worth finding out."

A smile tugged at the corners of my lips. God, how I wanted to believe him. It would be easy. Maybe the easiest thing ever.

It sounded like a stupid holiday movie. *Girl struggles to find job in the city. Girl goes home for Christmas. Girl falls in love with her high-school sweetheart, who has become a maturer version of his previous self with all the good looks still.*

Why did I want to turn him down?

Because ... because clearly, I was insane.

"Okay," I finally said, looking down at my hand, still held in his. "Let's see where it goes."

He grinned, the familiar spark in his eyes lighting up once more. "Good. Awesome. Good. I'll see you at the holiday party at the Huttons' tomorrow?"

I glanced up at the snow falling gently around us. "Yeah. I'll be there."

"I can't wait."

There could be a chance for something more again. Right?

I wanted to believe that.

That would be good. Easy. I had always liked Brenden. I *should* like him more than I liked Josh. Back in high school, I'd even entertained the thought of us growing up and getting married and everything, like anyone else might've with their semi-serious boyfriend, before we ended up moving in separate directions for college.

But if he was coming to the city for work? It almost seemed like it was meant to be.

That was what this kind of thing was one of those meant to be signs, wasn't it?

I just … needed to see if I could make my heart stop beating so hard in my chest and lips stop tingling whenever I thought of Josh.

twenty-six

"PLEASE DON'T BE mad at me." Gina clutched the throw blanket up to her chin like it was some kind of emotional armor.

Her eyes were wide with unabashed glee, but I could see it —the subtle flicker of nerves behind her grin. She actually thought I might yell at her for once in her chaos-stirring, charmed life. I should. I wanted to.

I'd had the whole walk home to prepare an argument, line up all the reasons why tonight was a mistake. Why she was out of line, why I couldn't handle this right now, why she should have never done this to me.

But instead, I just let out a breath and dropped my purse by the door of her bedroom.

"I'm not mad at you."

"You're not?" Her voice lifted with disbelief. "Really? Because after you left with him I had a good feeling that you totally were."

I shook my head, watching her as she lit up with the thrill of being right.

"You're not. You really aren't! Oh my God, come here and sit down and tell me everything. How did it go? What did he say? You have to tell me if he said something swoony. He still seems like the hopeless romantic type that wrote you cheesy love poetry."

I raised an eyebrow but let her tug me down to sit beside her on the bed and smooth part of her blanket over my lap. "Gina—"

"I heard rumors, okay?" she interrupted, eyes gleaming. "Like, actual, real-life gossip. That Brenden still talked about you. At alumni events. Like, wistful reminiscing. So, obviously, I did a little digging, and turns out, he wanted to see you. It felt … kind of fated, honestly."

"A second-chance romance?" I asked dryly, plucking at the edge of the blanket.

She grinned. "Exactly. Like, no messy breakup. No cheating. Just dumb high-school timing. You two were sweet together."

I didn't get the chance to respond. The sound of the front door opening and closing downstairs pulled both our gazes toward the footsteps coming up the stairs. Slow, familiar. Josh.

"You didn't answer me," repeated Gina. "How was it. Was it good? Bad?"

"What was good?" his voice paused, catching us as he passed Gina's doorway.

"None of your business," Gina said quickly, chipper and unbothered. "Our darling Bri, however, just went on maybe her only good date out of almost a dozen with the one and only Brenden."

My heart thudded.

"Because it was good, right?" Gina asked for the third time.

I felt Josh's gaze hit me before I even looked up, and when I did, I almost wished I hadn't. His eyes were already on me from where he stood halfway in the doorway, unreadable and impossibly steady.

"It was good," I admitted, voice low.

Her entire face lit up. "It was?"

"Your high-school boyfriend, Brenden?" Josh asked, interrupting again. Quiet. Just curious enough to sound harmless.

I swallowed hard, but my throat ached. "Yeah. It was nice to see him again."

There was a beat.

Josh nodded slowly. "Right. Of course." He didn't say anything else. Just turned and headed down the hall.

My eyes stayed on him until he disappeared.

"Niiight," Gina called after him without a care in the world.

She waited just long enough to hear Josh's bedroom door click shut before wriggling in place and turning toward me like a giddy kid at a sleepover. "Okay, now tell me everything that happened."

But I didn't say anything right away.

I didn't know how to tell her the part of where I still had spent half the evening thinking about someone else. Someone who had walked away tonight with a dullness in his eyes ever since I had left him standing alone at the gallery.

Brenden was good. Safe. Easy.

"Bri?"

"It was good," I said quickly again.

She cocked her head, giving me an odd smile. "Ok. Good. But I'm going to need more details."

* * *

I waited, lying in Gina's bed while she gently snored, until the rest of the house was still. I heard the telltale creak of the stairs and the hum of the dishwasher downstairs. I padded down the hall in my socks, holding my breath like it might somehow make this moment easier.

There, just like I'd known he would be—just like he was those years ago the last time I stayed with the Huttons for Christmas— sat Josh. Alone in the living room. His legs stretched out, a book resting open in his lap, though his thumb had stopped turning pages. His face was tilted toward the reading lamp, the soft amber glow catching the angles of his jaw and the faint crease between his brows.

"Hi," I said quietly, taking a seat beside him on the couch.

His gaze flicked to me without turning his head. "Hey," he said, then looked back down at the book.

After a pause, I reached out and gently took it from his hands, laying it on the coffee table as I sat down. "Josh, we need to talk."

This time, he looked at me directly. His eyes were tired, guarded. A little sad.

"About what?"

"About earlier," I said, tucking one leg under the other. "I know me seeing Brenden again probably wasn't expected."

He gave a slow nod. "It was a surprise, yes."

"A surprise." That was a good way to put it.

His jaw tightened even though his voice stayed maddeningly calm. "It's not like we're together, Brielle. You've said that pretty clearly. Several times. You don't need to give me any kind of excuse if that is what you are worried about here."

"I'm not giving you an excuse."

"Then why are you down here?" he asked.

I... That's not fair," I said softly.

"Isn't it?"

Silence fell between us like dust, thick and hard to shake. I felt him shift beside me, felt the way our shoulders accidentally brushed. At some point, I was watching his mouth again. God, I needed to stop doing that.

But Josh leaned in, just slightly, and my breath caught. He smelled like his eucalyptus bodywash again, something that made me think of that night on the couch and of everything we hadn't said since.

I swayed toward him.

And then he pulled back.

"You know what? I know where this is going here," he said suddenly, shaking his head. "We've already had this conversation. A few times now. I keep hoping you'll say something different, but you don't, and I can't keep having you tell me that you're not interested in something between us over and over again. I can't do it. Don't do it to me."

"Josh—"

"No," he cut in gently, almost like he didn't want to hear himself say it. "It's okay. You've been clear. I'm the one who wasn't listening. I'm the one still getting jealous enough that you come down here wanting to fix things. That's on me."

"You didn't—"

"I did." He ran a hand through his hair, then rested his arms on his knees. "But it won't be a problem much longer. I'm moving out in the new year, like I planned. We'll just ... clean-slate it. Pretend none of this ever happened."

"You're moving out." My voice was barely a whisper.

"That was always the plan, Bri." He didn't say it harshly, just with finality. Like the kind of truth that'd been sitting in your chest for a while, waiting for permission to breathe.

It was true. He'd said it before. I just hadn't really believed it until now. Or maybe I hadn't wanted to.

"Just be happy now, Brielle."

I looked at him, at the profile of the boy I used to sneak

glances at in high school. The man he'd become since. "Are you?"

He exhaled a long breath that seemed to pull from somewhere deeper than his lungs. His voice, when it came, was quiet enough to make me ache.

"I want to be."

12 THE
DATES TILL CHRISTMAS

BY BRIELLE THOMPSON

DATE ELEVEN

Location: My very own hometown.
First Impression: Let's all take a deep breath and try not to panic. Because Date Eleven — yes, ELEVEN — of my very ill-advised, very poorly planned blind date challenge just pulled the kind of plot twist even Hallmark would say is "a little on the nose."

My best friend set me up with my high school ex-boyfriend.

What are the odds, right? My best friend swore she was setting me up with "someone familiar but new." I didn't realize that translated to "your ex-boyfriend who looks exactly the same with less acne."

And here's the kicker: it wasn't awful. It was kinda nice. He's matured. He listens better. But here's the thing. I know what this is. This is Comfort. This is Familiar. This is the warm holiday sweater that smells like cinnamon and nostalgia and zero risk.

I guess what's wrong with that though, right?

I'm trying so hard to want someone and to make this worth something. Everything this season worth something. To want Date Eleven. Or at least to let myself want him.

Blind Date Status: Falling back into something easy is so much safer than falling into something that could ruin everything.

So yes, I said yes to a second date.

Maybe this was all meant to be in some sort of grand universe plan. Right?

twenty-seven

MRS. HUTTON FLITTED around the house with careful intention. She polished the holiday glassware and requested Mr. Hutton hang just a few more ornaments—ones she'd mysteriously rediscovered in a box labeled *Christmas '99* and insisted were crucial to the "overall aesthetic."

"It's classic!"

She clicked on every last strand of lights she'd carefully strung up earlier in the week until the entire house was glowing. Warm, welcoming. Blinding.

The kind of warmth that made me want to crawl into a corner and hide.

"Wear this."

I blinked down at the folded sweater Gina shoved into my hands. Forest green. Speckled with faint gold thread. Soft and festive. Just the right amount of cozy to scream, *I'm approachable, but not I'm in emotional chaos!*

I looked up. "Huh?"

Gina wiggled her eyebrows. "It'll look great. Especially for Brenden."

I rolled my eyes, but she caught my wrist and tugged me toward her bed.

"Sit. You've been weird all day."

"I'm fine."

"You've been ... I don't know. Extra quiet." She studied me like she could see the guilt forming a second skin beneath mine. "And you've been picking at your fingernails. You only do that when you're stressed or trying to lie to me."

"I'm just tired," I said. "You know how I am in a new bed."

"You sure that's it?" Her voice softened, the teasing gone.

For a flicker of a moment, I wanted to tell her everything. Lay it all out. Confess the emotional knots tied up inside me that connected between Josh, and Brenden, and everything I couldn't seem to make sense of.

Would it fix anything though? Would it release the weight or just ruin it all? Would I lose Gina too?

"Positive," I finally said, folding the sweater neatly across my lap.

"You've always been there for me. I just want to return the favor."

"I'm good, Gi. Really."

She gave me a look I knew too well. "Why do I feel like you're lying to me?"

"I'm not."

"Promise?"

My pulse tapped against my throat like a metronome.

Slowly, I nodded. "Promise."

"Okay." Her voice lightened again, giving me the out I had so clearly asked for. "Now put that on. I'll fix your hair, and we'll eat too many cookies, drink sangria, and pretend we don't make terrible decisions until the new year starts."

I smiled faintly. She grinned back, already shimmying into

her tartan skirt and holiday tights, looking like the cover of a vintage department store catalog.

* * *

Downstairs, the party was already in full swing.

The scent of cinnamon and cider hung in the air. Mrs. Hutton buzzed from room to room like a snowflake on a mission, collecting wine bottles and delivering compliments. Mr. Hutton grunted his hellos in between checking the thermostat and accepting cookies he clearly didn't want, but took anyway out of good manners.

I just tried to keep my hands warm inside the sleeves of my sweater and avoid eye contact with the front door.

"Brielle! Honey, how are you?"

Mrs. Jacobson from next door threw her arms around me. I got a faint whiff of Chanel No. 5 and peppermint schnapps.

I gave a polite smile.

Mr. Hutton, who had been lingering nearby, finally leaned in, voice low. "You all right, kid?"

"Yes. Thanks again for letting me come back for the holiday."

He gave me a look, one I couldn't quite read, then cleared his throat. "Don't thank me. You've always been here. Like one of the family."

My stomach tightened.

From the doorway came a sudden gust of cold and a burst of laughter. More guests arrived. Mrs. Hutton took the wine bottle offered to her like it was holy, bow and all.

Then there was Josh.

He came down the stairs just as the new guests filed in. His friends followed behind, faces vaguely familiar from high school, like blurry photos I couldn't quite refocus. He greeted them with a smile—that smile, the one that reached his eyes and had knocked the breath out of me once upon a time and apparently still did.

He wore a navy sweater that made his shoulders look broader. His hair was slightly damp, like he'd just stepped out of the shower. And then ...

He saw me. His eyes locked on to mine with that quiet, intense gaze I hated how well I knew.

The noise faded. Not in some romantic, fairy-tale way, but in that surreal, almost-cinematic pause that happened just before the floor gave out beneath you.

He kept walking. Closer.

I wanted to run. Not out of fear. But because I didn't trust myself not to say something, everything.

He passed by his friend with the shaggy hair and the girl in the red clip, and he didn't look away. Didn't even try to be subtle.

I couldn't stop looking either.

"Merry Christmas Eve, Brielle." Josh's voice was warm, yet there was something stilted about it, as if he was carefully measuring the space between us, like he was waiting for permission to move closer.

His eyes flicked between me and Gina, who was still fumbling with her hair bow, trying to keep it from flopping into her face every other step. The words lingered in the air between us, heavy with the quiet understanding that something had shifted—something unspoken yet entirely palpable.

His smile was genuine. It had always been, but his eyes ... they were different tonight. Searching. Thinking.

Neither of us was doing well with all this, were we?

My breath hitched, catching in my throat. The memory of that moment—the near brush of lips, the pull toward him that had felt so undeniable—was still fresh. I wasn't sure whether it was a mistake, a momentary lapse, or something deeper I couldn't ignore any longer.

"Good to see you again," I managed, my voice a little too thin, a little too quiet.

Gina, ever the interrupter, chimed in before I could let the silence stretch any further, "You literally just saw her at breakfast, you weirdo." She waved a dismissive hand, then shifted her attention to something else across the room. "Brenden's here already. How did you miss him? You should go talk."

She practically shoved me toward the direction of the party. "Gosh, it's like you're still clueless, even after all the dozen dates. You need to feed the person who likes you with your presence."

I could hear her in the background, but the mention of Brenden was enough to pull my attention entirely. My throat tightened as I caught sight of him across the room, standing there with a smile that was both familiar and foreign. He looked the same, but different in a way that made me ache.

"Your last date was with Brenden, wasn't it?" Mrs. Hutton's voice came from behind me, snapping me out of my haze.

Before I could even attempt to respond, Gina cut in with her signature dramatic flair. "They were practically perfect for each other," she said, her hands fluttering as if she were arranging us like dolls. "Forgive me for going with a classic romantic comedy trope. And he's smiling at you now." Gina gave me a nudge toward Brenden's direction. "Smile back!"

I could feel my lips stretch into a smile, but it felt like it was painted on, dry and brittle, like my red lipstick. The kind of smile that didn't quite reach my eyes.

Behind me, I could hear Mrs. Hutton's voice, light but filled with an almost-sharp curiosity. "Oh."

I glanced over my shoulder, catching her looking at me with a peculiar expression, one that said more than words ever could. It wasn't just a casual remark; it was something deeper, like she had noticed something in the air that I hadn't even recognized yet.

"Why *oh*, Mom?" Gina asked, oblivious to the underlying tension in her mother's tone as she waved her hand at me, trying to distract me with some new tidbit of holiday gossip.

But Mrs. Hutton's gaze never left me, sharp and attentive.

Her lips were slightly pursed, as though she was seeing something play out in front of her—a drama she hadn't expected to unfold.

Her eyes flicked quickly to Josh, who had just crossed the room, away from us, laughing at something with his friends, his carefree demeanor a stark contrast to the slow intensity building between me and Brenden.

I swallowed hard, trying to hold on to some semblance of control.

Mrs. Hutton cleared her throat softly, and in an instant, she was the image of politeness again, the facade of the perfect hostess slipping back into place.

"No reason," she said, though her voice betrayed a quiet curiosity that wasn't fully concealed.

I wasn't sure if she'd seen everything, but I felt the weight of her gaze like a soft pressure against my skin.

I stood there for a moment, my gaze fixed on Brenden. My heart beat a little faster. I was unsure whether to take the first step toward him or retreat back into the shadows. My body screamed to cross the room, to bridge that gap, to let him know that I was here. But my mind? My mind told me to stay.

I didn't need to say anything. His gaze was already there, waiting for me.

"Brielle?" he said softly, his voice grounding me in the chaos around us.

"I'm sorry," I whispered, the apology rising before I could stop it. It felt necessary, like I owed it to him.

Brenden paused before his shoulders slumped. God, was I that obvious? To everyone?

He gave a soft, understanding smile, his eyes lingering on me with a knowing softness. "I kind of figured something was up," he said, his voice a balm to the confusion swirling inside me.

I swallowed, my mouth suddenly dry. My words tangled in my throat, and I wasn't sure how to untangle them.

"It's just ..." I began, but stopped myself. What could I say to make it better? To explain everything without making it worse? "I'm sorry."

He shook his head gently, reading the hesitation on my face. "It's okay. Sometimes, high-school sweethearts are meant to stay in high school, right?" His voice softened, and a brief, almost-wistful laugh escaped him. "You guys had a thing a while back too. I remember the way he used to look at you. Back then, I thought it was weird. Now though ..." He let out a long breath. "Well, you look at him the same way, so ..."

His words stung in the best way possible, an acknowledgment of what we had once shared, but also a clear-eyed recognition that something had changed. It wasn't just about him anymore. It wasn't just about the past.

So ...

That was the word. The final word, and yet it felt like there was so much more hanging in the air between us. So ... what now? Where did this leave us?

"I really am sorry," I said again, trying to make my apology stick, to make it mean something.

"Don't be," Brenden said with a soft smile. "I wish you the best, Bri. Whatever that may be." His eyes flicked toward the crowd, the weight of everything shifting in the space between us. "We should catch up again. Sooner than this. Especially if I move out closer to you and Gina."

"Absolutely," I agreed, my voice tight but genuine. Part of me wondered if that was enough—if we could go back to being friends again after everything that had happened. But that was something I'd have to figure out later.

Brenden nodded once, then hesitated, as if considering whether to say something more. Instead, he shook his head with a quiet chuckle and turned to rejoin the group, not wanting to stretch the awkwardness longer than necessary.

I was thankful for that. Grateful even.

I watched him walk away, and with it, a strange relief washed over me.

I didn't need twelve dates or twelve guys to find Mr. Right. I only needed one. And I wasn't going to stop myself now before I reached him.

The thought settled in me like a comforting truth, warm and terrifying, all at once. I didn't know what the path ahead looked like, but I knew I had to take a step. Just one. Toward him.

So, I turned.

The sound of clinking glasses and muffled conversation rose around me as I threaded through the crowded living room, my eyes searching for that familiar figure. And then I saw him.

Josh stood in a small circle of people near the fireplace, the orange glow painting soft highlights in his dark hair. His mouth was curved in a real, easy smile—the kind he rarely gave out freely anymore—and it punched something deep in my chest. I felt it. The ache of almost.

She was standing beside him, laughing along with the group. A stunning woman with the kind of confidence that radiated naturally, her honey-blonde curls falling like they were styled for a commercial. And she was comfortable next to him. Effortlessly so.

I saw the way her eyes followed him as he took a sip from his glass, her gaze lingering, like she already knew the taste of him. And when she placed her hand lightly on his arm—fingers brushing, thumb tracing idle patterns back and forth as if she belonged there—I stopped walking.

Oh.

I froze mid-step, the breath caught in my throat.

That laugh. That casual touch. The familiarity. She looked at him like I sometimes caught myself looking at him when I forgot to be careful. And he … he didn't move away. He didn't pull back. He just … let her.

This was one of Josh's friends, wasn't it?

twenty-eight

I REMEMBERED her vaguely from before. It looked like I wasn't the only one getting back in touch with past significant others, was I?

But now she was here. In his space. With him.

As she should be. I mean, I didn't have any right to him. I'd told him we couldn't be anything, and now I ...

A sharp, slow ache built behind my ribs, something vulnerable cracking inside of me. I wasn't sure what I'd expected when I walked toward him. Resolution? Reassurance? Another near kiss we'd pretend never happened?

He glanced up, mid-laugh, catching my gaze. His smile faltered—not disappeared, just softened. Like he didn't know whether to hold on to it or let it go.

"Hey," he said, voice quiet despite the laughter around him. His eyes held mine with that frustrating depth that always made it feel like he could read me too easily.

The girl next to him looked between us, a small, polite smile forming as she stepped half a breath away, her hand sliding from his arm. "I'm going to grab another drink," she murmured, her voice kind and casual, but tinged with curiosity.

His focus was still entirely on me.

I took a step forward, still unsure what I was even doing, and offered a thin smile that didn't reach my eyes. "Hi."

"Hi," he echoed, his tone gentle now, edged with something quieter. A hesitation. "You okay?"

I nodded quickly. Too quickly. "Yeah. I just needed to see you for a second."

His eyebrows lifted slightly, and something flickered in his expression—hope maybe or surprise. "You found me."

"Yeah." My voice almost broke. "I found you."

And for a moment, we stood there, the air between us heavy. The girl hadn't gone far. She was just behind the punch table now, glancing over occasionally, and Mrs. Hutton, standing in the archway near the hallway, sipped her wine, but didn't look away.

I realized, all too suddenly, she was watching. Not just me. Us. Watching Josh. Watching me. Watching something.

Maybe she knew. Maybe she'd known all along.

Josh tilted his head, the noise of the party dimming around us.

"Do you want to talk?" he asked, his voice barely above a whisper.

"Yeah. I really do."

He took a slow step toward me, his fingers brushing mine in that quiet, unspoken way he always had—like he was asking permission without saying a word. And despite everything— his friend, the noise, the fear—I didn't pull away.

Not this time.

"Let's go talk," he said.

I nodded.

He took me down the hall toward his childhood bedroom. Growing up, I'd felt like it was a *do not enter* zone, both because of the fact that it was an extra turn down the hallway from the bathroom and also because of the sign he used to have posted there when he was in middle and high school. Now it was gone, and he led me right inside.

He shut the door behind us, the volume from downstairs decreasing dramatically.

"Are you okay?"

"Yes. No. I don't know."

He stared at me. " 'Cause you don't look okay, Brielle. And honestly, you are driving me crazy here."

"I'm driving you crazy?"

"Yes."

At least we were in the same zone.

"It was stupid," I told him, waving my hand around as if I could swat this entire problem away. Wow, I should've never come back to this town. So many things were meant to stay here, and I was dredging them all up. "I was stupid to even think that ..."

"To think what?"

"That you ..." Why was I struggling to say this?

He was leaving, and it would be just like it had been before he showed back up in my life and decided to become room-mates with me and Gina. So, what did it matter?

"That we ..."

Slowly, he nodded. Sighed. Sat down on the edge of his bed. The frame creaked.

He clapped his hands together. "You're ready now?"

"Ready?" I asked. Though it wasn't really a question.

Still, he answered, "Let's talk."

"We have."

"Really talk this time because, obviously, what we've been doing isn't working."

"It definitely isn't."

"I love you."

"Josh," I whined.

"What?"

"You were just downstairs with that girl."

"Kate?" He raised his eyebrows. "We were just chatting. My mom invited her and her family over. She's getting married next fall."

"Oh," I said softly, leaning from one foot to the other. What was it about Josh recently that made me feel like I was acting like a crazy teenager again? "I didn't ..."

"Wait. Brielle, were you jealous?"

"No. I was just ..."

His lip curled up. "You were jealous. You didn't realize it was Kate, and you thought—"

"You said you were already getting over me last night and—"

"You were jealous."

I didn't respond. I was jealous.

He shook his head. "Good."

"What?"

"Good. You're jealous. Fantastic."

"How's that good? From what I understand, jealousy isn't the best characteristic of a person."

He shrugged. "I don't care because for the past few days, that is all I've been thinking about."

"That I'm a newly jealous person?"

"How you were going to go off and meet someone else during your dates. Someone simpler. Easier for you and probably even smarter. And I was going to have to watch it happen," said Josh. "I probably still am. But what you're feeling right now is probably an ounce of what I have been dealing with while I tried to give you space to figure out how you'd play this."

I swallowed as my throat seemed to close. I took a deep

breath, trying to calm down my heart that really needed to chill out.

It was now or never.

I took a step forward, close enough that only a few inches separated us and the edge of the bed where he sat. The room felt impossibly small, filled with everything I hadn't said and everything I was suddenly ready to.

"I want you so badly that I feel like I'm going insane, Josh," I said, my voice raw with honesty. "You're always there. Everywhere. In my thoughts when I wake up. In my writing. I hear your voice in the back of my head asking, 'Why don't you write anything fun anymore?' Like you always used to."

He looked up at me, his eyes softening.

"And I've been trying," I went on, breath catching slightly, "even when it feels like the whole world is yelling *screw you* to anyone who isn't a doctor or a teacher or some perfectly polished adult with a benefits package and dental insurance. I've applied to a hundred terrifyingly boring desk jobs just so I don't drown."

"I know you have," he said gently. "Your newsletter is amazing, Brielle. It's funny and weirdly emotional, and it feels like ... you."

My heart stuttered. "You've read it?"

He gave a half smile. "I'm subscribed."

Somehow, that simple admission made my chest twist tighter. I pressed my lips together to hold back whatever wanted to pour out next—tears maybe. Gratitude.

Josh shifted slightly, the air between us thick with all the things we hadn't said until now. Then he asked quietly, "What about Brenden?"

I shook my head. "My story with Brenden ended a long time ago," I said, and it felt true. Firm. "And honestly? That's where it was supposed to end. He's a good guy. But it was high school. It never became anything more than that."

Something flickered across his expression. "Despite my sister's well-meaning schemes."

"Always so many well-meaning and chaotic intentions," I said with a faint smile, though my voice wavered.

"I'm just ..." I exhaled hard. "I'm scared of losing her. Of ruining the one constant person I've had. If things go bad between us—if this ends badly—what if everything else falls apart too?"

Josh stood slowly, closing the last of the distance between us. His hands came up to cradle my face, warm and steady, his thumbs brushing softly along my cheeks. "Hey, hey. Don't cry."

"I don't cry," I whispered, but my voice cracked. "I don't know what's wrong with me."

"There's nothing wrong with you." His eyes were searching mine now, serious and open. "It's okay to cry. It's okay to feel this. But I don't want to be the reason you're hurting."

"You're not," I said quickly. "It's me. It's all this inside me. I'm making it complicated because, in my head, it is complicated. Wanting something so badly when you're terrified of everything else falling apart? That's a special kind of hell."

"You're not going to lose everything, Brielle."

"How can you know that?" My voice came out sharper than I'd intended, my heart suddenly exposed like a nerve. "I've already lost so much."

He stilled, something changing in his expression. It was as if he finally saw the full scope of what I'd been carrying all these years.

"I tried—*I tried*—to build a life that had meaning anyway. I worked hard. I pushed through."

Josh didn't speak. He didn't interrupt. He just stood there, his hands on my face, holding me like I might shatter if he let go.

"I found Gina in school. She was loud and beautiful and didn't mind how quiet I was. I clung to her like a lifeline, and she never once made me feel like I was too much or too little. She let me stay here. She and her parents let me stay in this house, in this space, when I didn't have anywhere else to go. When home wasn't really home anymore. And this place ... this house became something safe. Something warm. It was good with Gina." I swallowed hard. "And it was good with you."

Josh's thumbs stilled on my cheeks.

"I hear you," he said at last, his voice barely above a whisper. "I won't pretend I know what that's like. I don't. I grew up in a stable house, with two parents who came to every school concert and every spelling bee. I went to college, made a safe choice, then left it all when I realized being happy mattered more than being practical. But you?" He paused, shaking his head like he couldn't quite believe I was standing in front of him. "You made something out of nothing. You built yourself from scraps and still turned into someone beautiful and strong and wildly good."

My eyes welled with tears again.

"That's what I love about you, Brielle," he said, his voice catching. "Not perfection. Not the strength even. But the way you keep going when it would be so easy to stop. You still want. You still hope."

I let out a shaky breath.

"That's what I love about you."

twenty-nine

"LOVE?"

He chuckled. "Mmhmm." He didn't deny the word. He only continued, "I will do whatever I can to make sure that Gina doesn't get angry, Brielle. But it sounds to me that you need to make your own choice even if it's hard. You deserve to have a life that is perfect for you. Even if it makes things hard sometimes."

His soft brown eyes never left mine. "And we need to have fun while making those choices."

And the last time I'd had fun was with him. On our first not-date. At the gift-wrapping table at the school fundraiser. Watching new television shows. Every time I was with him.

Once, I had been brave and maybe a little stupid to immediately go after what I wanted just a few years ago. Was I going to be brave again?

Brave enough for the both of us?

"Tell me, Brielle. Tell me what we are going to do. Because right now, all I want to do is kiss you and tell you that I love you again because it feels like the best thing I've ever said."

I wanted him to do that too.

Josh went on. "I want to lay you down on this bed and take away any uncertain, scared thoughts you have and tell you everything is going to be all right. I'm going to make sure of it, and these days, I've been keeping my promises. I'm also trying not to live with regrets, and I have a feeling that if you walk away again, Brielle, losing you will be the biggest regret of my life."

"What if Gina is angry? What if ..."

"She'll get over it," he said. "Gina says she holds grudges, but really, we both know she has a limited attention span for it."

She also had a soft heart. I mean, even the fact that we had somehow moved in together, like our plans from when we had been kids, said something, didn't it? On and off phone calls and checking in over the years, and yet still ... here we were. I had to have faith maybe she would understand. Maybe it would all end up okay, and if it didn't ...

I thought losing Josh would be the biggest mistake I'd ever made, and I felt like I had been making a whole lot of those in the past year as I figured my life out on my own. And if this was another one?

So be it.

"I don't want to lose you either, Josh," I said. "Do you promise ..."

"I promise."

I sniffed a laugh. "You haven't even heard what I was going to say."

"I don't care. My heart is going to give out at this rate, and I know whatever you say, I'll want it back tenfold. You want me to promise to take care of you? Done. You want me to promise that this isn't some phase or fun for me again? Double done. You want me to promise to love you? I have a good feeling that is already ingrained in stone, considering I've already been doing that for a long time now. Longer than I want to admit. But it's time for both of us to do things for us. I promise I'll help you with that too. Whether it is cooking or writing or whatever. I promise to be there for you. Do you promise not to give up on me?"

I took a deep breath, and it hung between us before I smiled. "I promise."

Still holding my face, Josh brushed his lips over mine in a breath before they pressed down hard against mine.

Whatever kiss we'd had back at the apartment had nothing on this one. It was pure and strong, and I needed everything it gave me.

Because it made me know one thing.

This was real. And Josh and me?

The way he gripped on to me, hands smoothing down my body, reaching for the bottom of my sweater, told me he was on the exact same page as I was now. There was nothing to hold back. There was no reason to.

"I've loved you for a long time, Josh," I said. "Don't make me regret it."

"I'll spend every day making sure you don't."

Another kiss, another touch.

At some point, the sweater I had borrowed from Gina ended up on the floor, leaving me in my bright purple bra. The back of my legs hit the edge of the bed. Josh guided the way, and I was only wondering how we weren't already on it as I lifted a knee to wrap around his hip.

"Are you sure?"

"Are you sure?" I asked right back. "Because I'm sure. I'm done not being sure. I've never wanted anything more than you right now. I've never wanted anyone as much as I want you, Josh. In case I haven't already spilled my entire heart open for you more than a couple of times, whatever happens, I'm going to choose you. I don't need any more dates. You're it."

I couldn't help it. Even though I was breathless, I laughed.

Smiling right along with me, he nodded.

His hand reached up to cup the side of my face, and he kissed me hard again before breaking away. "I am sure. More than sure. I want you so bad, Brielle. I want you more than I've ever wanted anything."

I took his thin sweater in my hands and pulled it over his head.

I went for his belt next.

He followed my lead with an easy swipe, releasing the hooks on my bra and the button on my suddenly-too-tight jeans. Air hit my chest, and my nipples hardened as he licked his lips.

"I've wanted you for a long time. And I've been patient. But please, if you have any mercy on my stupid self after all this time, don't make me wait any longer."

Twisting me so that I straddled his legs, he pulled me tight against him. I felt his length rub against me, and I gasped at the sensation. The rest of my body was in a state of shock still, thrilled and excited and unbelieving that this could possibly be happening.

My hands shook as I braced myself on his chest.

"Take me, Brielle," he said. "Be the brave one between the two of us. You always have been."

"Condom?"

He smiled. "Top drawer."

He reached out, and the nightstand drawer opened with a creak much louder than either of us expected. He shuffled his hand around inside until he found a box that looked like it hadn't been touched in a long time.

"Are those even still good? They look like they are from high school."

Flipping the package around, he nodded. "Not that old. And success. Not expired. Thank God. Looking for a way out?"

I shook my head, reaching out to drag him back toward me by his belt loops. "Trying to make you move faster."

Luckily, Josh didn't struggle as he stripped me the rest of the way and let his own jeans fall to the floor with them. He opened the foil package and slipped the condom onto himself, letting my hands guide him.

He groaned, "I need all of you."

"You're going to have me." *I'm going to have you.*

Would it be appropriate right now to say, *Once and for all, finally*?

Josh's eyes locked with mine as he positioned himself between my legs. His gaze was intense as he let out a deep breath. He tenderly traced the contours of my face before leaning in to softly kiss me once more, his lips lingering gently on mine. "I don't know how long I'm going to last with you."

"I don't care," I whispered.

We didn't need to be loud anymore. There was such little space between us, and the only noise I was focused on wasn't the party downstairs, but the heavy thrum of Josh's heartbeat in his chest, which I rested my hand over.

"I just want you."

We kissed again like we were making up for all the days we had spent pretending our feelings weren't what they were for each other—every year, day, hour, second—our breaths became shallow and irregular. Whatever had happened in the days, weeks, or years to come, none of it could compare to this moment.

As Josh entered me, I cried out, even as he whispered in my ear, "God, you feel better than my dreams."

I let out a deep moan, my hands immediately clutching on to his broad shoulders for support. He looked down at me with a mix of love and lust in his eyes. He was a sight, bare like this, perfectly fitting against me. I never wanted to forget it. Ever.

Our bodies moved against each other at a rapid pace, as we knew that right now was not the time for languidness. That was for later. A good thing, considering I wasn't sure if I could stand it slow and steady as the sensation of him inside of me felt like electricity, sending me higher with every movement that my hips rose to meet. I was dizzy with desire.

Josh gently brushed my hair, threading his fingers in it and sending shivers down my spine. "You're so beautiful. So perfect for me."

I wrapped my arms around his neck, pulling him closer.

"I love you too, Josh," I whispered.

His eyes locked on to mine, and I saw a mix of emotions—love, passion, and was that the all-too-familiar hint of worry?

"Don't look so scared," I said, trying to lighten the mood. "I trust you."

"I'm not scared. Not anymore" He paused for a moment, looking deep into my eyes. "I'm ready."

"For what?"

"Everything, so long as I'm with you."

I held him tighter as the weight of his words settled upon us. Our bodies continued to move fast and in unison, our breaths entwined. I felt like I was shocked into motion, taking as much as I could, until we both gasped. I tensed and cried out against his sharp moan.

"Josh." I shuddered.

"I got you." He breathed heavily, holding me through my peak until I was all the way back down with him again. "I got you."

thirty

"EVERYONE'S GOING TO KNOW NOW," I murmured as I curled into Josh's chest, still breathless, still not quite believing what had just happened between us.

Josh's fingers trailed gently up and down my spine, grounding me in the aftermath. "Don't worry," he said, pressing a kiss to the top of my hair. "I'll be right by your side. I promised, didn't I?"

One by one, we started pulling ourselves back together—pants tugged on, sweaters smoothed out. I tried to move efficiently, but my gaze kept drifting back to him. I couldn't help it. I stared at the freckle tucked in the slope of his shoulder, the slight dimple above his hipbone, the curve of muscle along his lower back, which I made a mental note to revisit when we weren't hiding upstairs during a family Christmas party.

Josh caught me staring and smirked. "Not tonight though."

"Not tonight," I echoed with a sigh, though I didn't look away. "Think anyone's noticed we've been gone?"

"Eh," he said, shrugging as he buckled his belt, "not unless they're paying attention. Though I'm pretty sure my mom already knows."

I straightened, surprised. "What?"

He shot me a knowing look. "She keeps slipping your name into every conversation. Like, 'Is Brielle still writing her news-letter?' Or, 'Brielle likes those cookies, remember?' It's been ... frequent."

I frowned. "You think she knows?"

"I think anyone with eyes could tell how completely in love I am with you."

The air caught in my throat. I stared at him, lips parted, suddenly less concerned with how my sweater was still half untucked and more concerned with the fact that I might melt into the floor.

We definitely didn't have time for another round, but when his eyes crinkled with that sparkle, playful and sincere, I felt myself wanting to throw caution—and my jeans—to the wind.

I shook my head, grinning. "Where's your belt?"

He glanced around.

I spotted it on the other side of the room and tossed it toward him. "Here."

"Thanks."

"Anytime."

"For the belt or for the sex?" he teased, eyes glinting as he threaded it through the loops.

I raised a brow. "Are you thanking me for the sex?"

"Oh, I'll be thanking you for that for the rest of my life—if you'll let me."

I blushed furiously, trying to regain any shred of composure I had left. "We really need to go downstairs before people start wondering if we died."

Josh nodded, but the way his eyes lingered on me said he wasn't ready to stop looking just yet. "Do you see my shirt?"

"Um." I looked around on the floor. I was still tucking my

sweater into the front of my jeans when I heard the last few footsteps come down the hall and push open the door.

"Bri? Are you in there? Brenden said—"

And froze.

Gina stood there, mid-step, her face slack with shock. Her eyes bounced between us—from my flushed face to Josh's still-unkempt hair to the barely concealed guilty expression we both wore.

Then her gaze locked on me.

Her chest rose visibly, like she was trying to inhale enough air to make the moment make sense.

"What ..." she asked slowly, voice pitching high at the end. "What am I looking at right now?"

thirty-one

"OH MY GOD. What am I looking at?" The same voice said the three words again before I managed to respond to it.

Or think about responding to it.

Josh was already striding forward to block me. "Gina."

"No." She put out a hand toward him, turning her face away from the two of us. "I don't even … *no*. You're not serious. You two—*here*—*now*—during the *Christmas party*? You're not even dressed, so I don't want to look at you right now. Fix that."

I swore her eye twitched.

"Oh my God," she repeated. "You're sleeping with my brother?"

Josh raised his hand sheepishly. "Technically … we just finished."

"Joshua!"

He winced both from the pitch of his sister's voice and the way I swatted him. "Sorry. That felt funnier in my head."

I stepped forward, reaching for Gina's arm. "Gina, I'm so sorry. We were going to tell you. It just … happened."

"Clearly." Her eyes narrowed again.

Blinking, she shook her head, already turning away.

"Gina!" I called after her, but she was already moving.

Finally, near her room, she stopped.

"Sorry, I just ... I need some literal space between whatever —well, not *whatever* was happening in there. I'm pretty sure I know what was happening, and now I'm very grateful that one of our nosy neighbors distracted me for an extra five minutes about what exactly an art gallery museum person did so that I didn't walk in on you two doing exactly what I know you were doing in there." She waved her hand back down toward the hallway.

I glanced back there, too, seeing the light still on for Josh, who was still probably trying to find his shirt.

"You two were ..." Gina drifted off. She didn't want to say it, but it was clear she needed to repeat it to herself a few times before it fully sank in.

So much for Josh and I waiting to tell everyone.

To tell Gina.

I tried to figure out how to fix this, but nothing was coming to mind. There was nothing to fix, and yet the way Gina's face was screwed up as she worked through what was going on said otherwise.

"I'm—" Where did I begin? "I'm sorry I didn't say something before, Gina."

"He's my brother, Bri."

"I know."

I imagined my face was flushed and lips swollen. So much so that she had to shut her eyes again.

She took a deep breath.

"I'm really sorry, Gina. I know I shouldn't have, and I should've said something maybe sooner, but—"

"You really like him," she said.

I didn't answer, a little taken aback.

"For how long?"

"Not terribly long. Not exactly." The words felt like an excuse, but I didn't know how else to explain it.

She let out a slow breath, rubbing her temples like she was trying to piece it all together. "I thought I'd noticed it, back at the apartment, but I dismissed it. Thought I was just over-thinking things, seeing things that weren't there. I thought you and Josh were finally being nice to each other, you know, like friends or something—maybe because you'd felt guilty or because I'd kept pushing you two to make amends."

I shook my head, trying to keep it together.

"It's been going on the whole time?" she asked again, the confusion in her voice making it clear how out of place this all felt.

"Not the whole time." I gave the simplest answer, hoping it would cut through the tension.

Her eyes flicked between me and the floor, her mind working through everything. "For how long have you been ... have you been sleeping with him in the apartment?"

"No," I said quickly, my eyes squeezing shut, as if the words themselves were too much. "No, we didn't do anything there. Things just got complicated, and then ... no. This was the first time."

She was silent for a moment, just taking it in. Then she let out a breath, her face softening. "Really?"

I nodded, and for a second, it almost felt like I was giving her a confession. A small, quiet truth.

Her brow furrowed slightly. "But you liked him. You always have. And I could tell. When I walked in on you two the other day ... your hair was ..." She trailed off, her voice catching as the pieces started to fall into place.

I opened my eyes, finally looking at her. There was no way out of this anymore.

"Yes. Sort of. I mean, we were just kissing." The last part felt awkward, like a lie, but it was the truth. Or at least, it was all I could give her right now.

But we had just kissed.

And touched.

And wanted to do a whole lot more if I was remembering my reaction correctly.

She seemed to deflate a little, but the uncertainty was still there. I couldn't tell if it was anger or disappointment—maybe a mix of both. But it wasn't the blowup I'd expected. She wasn't yelling or berating me. She was just … processing.

Her eyes flickered away from mine for a moment, and then she sighed. "I feel like I missed something huge here, something that's been going on this whole time."

I waited for her to say something, for her to tell me more of what she was really thinking. Was she going to ask me to leave? To pack up and go home? Would she kick me out of the apartment, out of her life entirely? I stood there, waiting and waiting for the inevitable.

"You like my brother."

"Yeah."

"Like you *really* like him?"

I nodded. "I do."

"You just had sex with my brother, wearing my sweater."

To be fair, the sweater had come off, but I did cringe for her. "Sorry about that."

She didn't seem very concerned about it anymore as a new thought came to her. "And he likes you too," she said. "He's not just messing with you."

I shook my head. "I mean, I hope not."

"He carried you to your room whenever you fell asleep on the couch back at the apartment."

"You saw that?" I asked. I hadn't thought that she was

home back then in the beginning when her work really started to amp up.

"Yeah. I did. The way he looks at you ..." She sighed. "He used to look at you that way too. Years ago, when we were all in high school and even after he came back from college. He always asked about you and how you were doing. I'm really stupid, aren't I?"

"No, Gina. Of course not."

"Well, this sucks."

"You're mad?"

"Oh, I'm mad," she said. "Mostly, I'm just mad you didn't tell me. And because now I owe Mom twenty bucks."

I choked. "Wait, what?"

"She said she'd give it till Christmas. I told her she was nuts." Gina sighed, her voice taking on a more serious tone, "You know, I haven't been there for you."

"You have. You helped to set me up on all the dates."

"Please, we both know that you wouldn't have done that on your own unless you felt guilty enough to keep going."

"You helped me get back out there and write actual decent words again, and it has felt really good. Readers even like it. More than I thought, honestly, which I still do not understand. Some of them are even paying to read it twice a week."

"They are?" she asked with a gasp.

"Yeah," I said.

"That's amazing, Bri!"

"Thank you. But you helped me get to this point. Thank goodness or else I wouldn't be able to pay rent next month."

"So, you'll still want to live with me?"

"What?"

"When you and my brother get together and live happily ever after, you'll still want to live with me?" she asked. "Because, for some ungodly reason, he chose now to come back, and I'm pretty sure he's going to stick around, fixing projectors and other nonsense at a school that undervalues him for maybe the rest of his life."

She looked directly at me as she said the next part. "More than sure now."

"Of course I'll want to live with you."

"Not forever, of course. But you know what I mean."

"I mean, you are going to find a big millionaire art buyer and let him sweep you off your feet any day now."

"You know I will," she insisted, as if I was joking. "But I want to say this now, however late. Okay?" She bolstered herself. "You don't have to hide anything from me. If you like him ... ... well, it's okay."

"You really aren't mad?"

Taking a deep breath again, she shook her head. "Nope. I don't ever want to hear anything about what goes down between you two though. Already, this was a bit much. Got it?"

"Got it."

"Good," she agreed. "Glad we are on the same page. You deserve to be happy. Even if it is with my brother. Kind of gross, but you've done everything for me, even now, when we are all over the place and I'm so busy. I'm going to support you. But if something goes wrong and my brother messes this up with you, I—"

"Nothing will ever tear you and me apart."

She let out a sigh that looked like she'd been holding on to it for a while. Relief.

"Good. Because you're always my best friend, Bri. Whether or not he's your soulmate or whatever, you're mine."

thirty-two

"I GUESS this could all work out. We'll be, like, actual sisters now," declared Gina.

"Don't get ahead of yourself," I said, though I'd also thought about that. Maybe a few times.

She laughed loudly over the holiday music rising up to greet us as we walked down the steps. I glanced down the hall as we went, noting Josh's bedroom light had turned off. He returned to the holiday party as if he never left. He stood near the fireplace, engaged in a lively conversation with a group of his friends.

"You go," said Gina. "I'm going to get a drink. I need one."

I smiled, watching her go.

As I made my way over to him, our eyes met and a warm smile spread across his face. It was a smile that held unspoken promises and reassurances, making my heart flutter despite the playful banter with Gina echoing in my mind.

I paused in my steps as one of his friends pushed him playfully, not wanting to interrupt yet.

Luckily, someone else came up alongside me. "We're glad you're here."

Turning to the side, I looked up at Mrs. Hutton.

"We're always glad you're here and can call this place home, but I'm very glad," she said. "Because it looks like you've brought him home too."

"Oh, I didn't ..."

She shrugged with a sip of her wineglass. "Either way, I don't think I've seen him smile like that since he was a boy."

I looked over to where he opened his mouth and laughed at something someone had said. I wanted to see it, soak in that sound and smile forever.

"Thank you."

I wasn't sure how to process it all.

Everyone was happy, and I was too. I was ...

Josh glanced over at me with another smile before going back to the conversation with his friends.

I think I needed a minute.

Walking through the party, I grabbed my coat from where I had left it in the laundry room.

I paused, remembering squeezing with Josh between the wall and dryer the last time I was here at the Huttons before I opened the door to outside. It was quiet. The steady music behind me in the house was only a few trill notes escaping through the sliding glass door here and there.

The ice felt like a shot to my lungs.

I couldn't help it; I turned around the corner and took another minute.

And another as I walked.

* * *

I stood in front of the small house with the metal fence, a quiet chill settling into my bones. There were little candles flickering in the windows, casting soft, golden glows that made the house feel oddly welcoming. But the house didn't bother with Christmas lights, not like it used to. Yet, in some strange way, it felt more homely now. How odd, after all these years, I never imagined it could feel this way. I'd spent so long convincing myself it could never be home. At least, not for me.

Yet now, as I stood here, detached but somehow at ease, the place felt different. It wasn't the house. It was me.

"Honestly, this wasn't the first place I thought I'd find you."

The voice startled me, and I turned to see Josh walking up alongside me. There was a wave of relief that followed quickly after my surprise. He'd found me. He had come after me.

"Where did you try first?" I asked, trying to sound casual, but I was grateful he was here.

"Gina's bedroom. The laundry room. That felt like a classic. Then I thought I'd check the backyard in case you were suddenly inspired to make snow angels."

I couldn't help but smile, even as I shook my head. "That might've been a better idea."

He grinned, the corners of his eyes crinkling with affection. "That's when I saw the tiny footprints on the sidewalk and figured I'd give here a try. So ... what are you doing here?"

"I know I should probably get back to your mom's party," I said, my voice more of a whisper than I'd meant it to be.

Josh didn't immediately respond. He just looked at me for a moment, as if assessing my mood, the way I held myself. "Didn't say that. I want to know if you're okay. It's been a lot tonight."

I chuckled softly, tucking a loose strand of hair behind my ear. "It has."

We both stood there, the weight of the silence surrounding us like a blanket. It wasn't uncomfortable though. It was ... soothing. The only sounds were our deep, even breaths and the hum of the neighborhood around us. Despite the cold in the air,

I felt something warm spreading through me, just knowing that Josh was here beside me.

"I didn't think I'd ever want to come back to this place," I said, breaking the silence. "I didn't spend a lot of time here when I was younger. Between school, extracurriculars, and … well, your house. Eat, sleep, repeat."

I glanced at the house again, this time seeing it in a new light, the old bricks and small details becoming more familiar. Maybe it wasn't so shabby after all.

"You did spend a lot of time at our place," Josh said softly, looking at me as if he could sense my thoughts. "I never really knew how bad it was for you."

"It wasn't bad," I said quickly, shaking my head. "Not exactly. It just … was a challenge."

He reached for my hand, his fingers warm as they wrapped around mine. "And you're brilliant at taking them on. Even when you shouldn't have to."

I gripped his hand tighter, feeling his warmth seep into me. He pulled both of our hands into the pocket of his lined coat, holding me close before we headed back the way I came. Eventually we were back in front of the Hutton house—our real house in a way. The one I knew better than any other.

The house was lit up with white lights, people trickling out of the party, carefully picking their way over the ice that had started to form on the driveway. There was a soft cheer in the distance, a laughter-filled murmur that made me smile.

"I'm ready to go back in," I said, my voice steady now.

"You sure?" Josh asked, his tone laced with gentle concern.

I squeezed his hand. "Yeah, I'm sure."

We started walking together, side by side, toward the front door. Josh's pace in step with mine, like he was in no rush to leave, but also didn't want to waste any time. I could feel the way he was watching me, still assessing, still trying to understand all the things I couldn't say yet. But there was no rush for those answers either.

We stood in front of the Hutton house, watching the last of the party guests leave, their laughter trailing behind them like echoes of the night.

I started, my voice low, "This has always been my home. With you."

Josh smiled, his eyes softer now. "Thanks for waiting for me."

I leaned into him, resting my head on his shoulder for a brief moment, feeling the warmth of him seep through me. "Thanks for being brave."

His voice dropped, just a little, filled with an intensity that made my heart beat faster. "I'm never going to let you go again, Brielle. Don't even think about it."

I pulled back, looking up at him, my brow furrowing in disbelief. "You mean that?"

"Where was it not clear that I'm already completely in love with you?"

The words landed in my chest like a small, precious weight, one I hadn't known I needed until now. "It was."

"Good."

He said it again, his voice warm and at peace, like a melody that was meant just for me. He leaned down and kissed my cheek, his lips grazing my skin, a gentle promise.

I turned to face him fully now, feeling the weight of everything between us.

I studied his face for a long moment, just taking him in. "You're not going to get bored of me though? Not going to get bored of the city, get nervous that you're not living enough, and just ... leave me?" The questions slipped out before I could stop them, the fear creeping in like it always did. Fear of being left alone again.

Josh's expression softened, his hands sliding down my arms until they found mine, holding them gently. "I have a feeling you'll be my best adventure, Brielle. Our best adventure."

I cupped his hands tightly. I wasn't going to let him get away. Not this time.

"You know what I think though?"

"What?"

He grinned just as brightly as the Christmas lights, and I soaked him in with utter awe of how we had gotten here.

"I think we should probably go on a date first."

12 THE DATES TILL CHRISTMAS

BY BRIELLE THOMPSON

DATE TWELVE

Location: Home.
First Impression: Your first impression of him was in Date One.

To those of you who have loyally followed my Twelve Blind Dates of Christmas...

This is it. The final chapter. The last date. And a big reveal.

And to the four of you who messaged me with, "What about the best friend's brother? He seems cute??" after his brief, cameos...

Well. You were right. He is cute. Annoyingly, unfairly cute. And, maybe worse, he's kind. And funny. He was never supposed to be in the running. He was just my best friend's brother that yes, I've had a crush on since high school.

I didn't think much of it. Or at least I pretended not to. Because falling for him felt too... obvious. Too close. Too real. I've been doing my absolute best to avoid real this whole time so not to mess everything else in my life up.

So, yeah.

I didn't end the Twelve Dates of Christmas with a stranger. I ended it with someone who's known me longer than any of the others. Who didn't need to be set up to see me, because he's been seeing me the whole time.

Blind Date Status: To those of you rooting for him since the beginning, congratulations. You win.

And honestly? So do I.

THE
DATES TILL CHRISTMAS

BY BRIELLE THOMPSON

HI READERS,

Remember Date Five? The one where I unknowingly walked into a dive bar and discovered my date was trying to juggle two women at once in the same building, and left early with the other girl in his dating rotation?

Turns out, in addition to being deeply cool. She also works in publishing.

Fast forward a few chaotic months, a lot of emails, one emergency copy deadline fueled entirely by cinnamon rolls and nervous breakdowns, and — surprise! — I got a book deal.

The 12 Dates Till Christmas is officially going to be a real, physical book. With pages! And chapters! And, unfortunately, everything I ever wrote about my digestive system on Date Six!

So for those of you who laughed, cringed, messaged me *"girl, no,"* or rooted for my best friend's brother without knowing you were 100% correct the whole time — this book is for you.

And it's proof that sometimes the worst dates can lead to the very best stories.

You can preorder it now (!!!) using the link below.

Thank you for following along, for cheering me on, and for never once telling me to give up even when I maybe should have, somewhere around Date Four.

This isn't goodbye. It's just... *Chapter One.*

acknowledgments

Writing 12 Dates Till Christmas has been a cozy little adventure —kind of like the dates Brielle has to go through in this book. It's an adventure of hardship, determination, and most of all hope.

In my case, the hope to write one more book.

And here we are.

Though I didn't have a long list of people behind the scenes, I'm grateful for the quiet moments and late nights that helped bring this story to life.

First and foremost, thank you to the most important people in my life for your constant support, patience, and overall encouragement throughout this journey. You know who you are. This book's and all the others that have been written and will be written. Your love has been my foundation and pushes me forward towards this dream of mine.

To my editor, Jovanna, thank you for your sharp eye, kind guidance, and steady hand in shaping this book into its final form. Your insight and marvelous editing skills make all the difference.

And finally, to the readers who pick up this book, thank you so much. Whether you love a good best friend's brother romance, enjoy a slow burn, or just want a holiday escape, I hope this story brings you a little joy and sparkle this season.

Happy reading.

about the author

Kendra Mase is the author of emotional, romantic, sometimes magical stories including *Call You Mine* and *Bewitched by You*. You can visit her online at kendramase.com.

also by kendra mase

ASHTON

The Strings That Hold Us Together

Everything You Never Had

Words That Burn Like Ash

The Way We're Meant To Be

BARNETT WITCHES

Bewitched By You

Put a Spell on You

HOME HAVEN

When in December

STANDALONE

12 Dates Till Christmas

Call You Mine

www.ingramcontent.com/pod-product-compliance
Lightning Source LLC
Chambersburg PA
CBHW030112260626
47156CB00008B/2625